PRO SE ✠ PRESS

THE GUNSMITH #410: SILENT ASSASSIN
A Pro Se Press Publication

THE GUNSMITH #410: SILENT ASSASSIN is a work of historical fiction. Many of the important historical events, figures, and locations are as accurately portrayed as possible. In keeping with a work of fiction, various events and occurrences were invented by the author.

Edited by Tommy Hancock
Editor in Chief, Pro Se Productions—Tommy Hancock
Submissions Editor—Rachel Lampi
Director of Corporate Operations—Kristi King-Morgan
Publisher & Pro Se Productions, LLC-Chief Executive Officer—Fuller Bumpers

Cover Art by Jeffrey Hayes
Print Production and Book Design by Percival Constantine
New Pulp Logo Design by Sean E. Ali
New Pulp Seal Design by Cari Reese

Pro Se Productions, LLC
133 1/2 Broad Street
Batesville, AR, 72501
870-834-4022

editorinchief@prose-press.com
www.prose-press.com

Published in digital form by Piccadilly Publishing,

THE GUNSMITH

#410 SILENT ASSASSIN

J.R. ROBERTS

PRO SE ⚖ PRESS

ONE

Colorado

Clint Adams enjoyed many things in life: A cool drink on a hot day. The sound of poker chips as they clattered against each other while being raked toward him. The touch of wind against his face as he rode on a long stretch of open trail. One thing he enjoyed was something he'd picked up from his youth and that was working with his hands.

By trade, Clint was a gunsmith. He knew his way around damn near anything that sent a bullet through a barrel at a quick enough pace to do some damage. Although it was his craft and had earned him no small amount of respect, it was how he put those firearms to use that had spread his name through certain circles of a rough and violent world. Clint was never one to shy away from anything, but it did feel good to ride somewhere he wasn't immediately recognized as a gun hand. Instead, he earned his keep like any other man; through hard work and perseverance.

When he'd first arrived in Colorado, Clint was tired and somewhat angered that a swollen river had washed out the bridge he'd meant to take. Thanks to an adjustment to his route, he'd been forced to ride into some of the roughest country he'd seen since the last time he'd crossed the Rocky Mountains. It had tacked on three extra days to his ride and steered him well clear of the destination he'd originally had in mind. As he rode into the first town he'd spotted, Clint didn't figure on staying long enough to bother learning its name. That was nearly three weeks ago, however, and in that time Celia Flats had grown on him.

As far as town went, Celia Flats was a mess. Some of those differences were simply because Clint had grown accustomed to settlements that were newer and mostly utilitarian by nature. They were spread out, easy to navigate and mostly open. While Celia Flats was certainly open, it had the meandering, sprawling feel of a town that had sunk its roots several decades ago and spread in random directions like moss growing on the side of a tree. Once Clint decided to stay in town for a spell, those differences became much easier to bear.

Being within a stone's throw of the Colorado River, Clint could hear the water and, when the wind blew the right way, smell it. Some of those experiences were better than others and they all became even more enjoyable once he'd gotten his first sip of George's Red Brew.

George's was a saloon named after a beer that was brewed by its owner. The sign bearing its name had caught Clint's eye when he'd first ridden into town. The beer was strong enough to keep him from riding away that night and tasty enough to keep him coming back for more. Unfortunately, it kept flowing to such a degree that Clint found himself playing Faro when he knew all too well it was a game that was damn near unwinnable. Bucking the tiger was a fool's pastime and Clint felt like an awfully big fool when he'd lost close to a hundred dollars in one night. The owner of the saloon was understanding and gave Clint a bit of time to square his account, since Celia Flats had no bank and he couldn't access his money. One of the ways that was suggested for him to raise some money was to work at one of the more prosperous businesses in Celia Flats.

Callum Parts & Supply Company was located at the edge of town closest to the river. Over a game of poker, Clint spoke to a few men who worked there about the place and any prospects for employment. They were friendly guys who loved to talk just as much as they loved playing cards.

"So tell me something about this place?" Clint asked, looking at the five cards in his hands.

"Callum's?" Kelly Fox said, with a grin. "Ol' Ed, he's a good guy to work for."

"He's a little cranky, though," Ben Dover added. "Cards, Adams?"

Clint took three cards out of his hand and tossed them.

"I'll take three."

Dover dealt him the cards.

"Kelly?"

"One."

Fox had a habit of trying to fill straights, especially with belly cards. Clint wasn't worried about him.

The third player took two. His name was Rance Quaid. He'd drifted into the saloon about an hour before. Nobody knew him, but he decided to fill the empty chair in the game. From the condition of his clothes, he was riding the trail and had been for some time. He was just passing time and was not a very good card player.

"Dealer takes three," Dover said.

Clint had drawn a third ace to the two he'd been dealt. Looking at the other men's faces, and body language, he felt sure he had the winning hand.

But it had been Fox that opened—with nothing, Clint was sure.

"Kelly?" Dover asked.

"Ten dollars."

"Quaid?"

The stranger scowled and tossed his cards down toughly. "I fold."

"I call," Dover said. "So, you lookin' for Callum, Mr. Adams?"

"No," Clint said, "never heard of him before today, but I'm just looking for something to do. I raise twenty."

"You saw me take one, right?" Fox asked.

"I did."

"Then I raise twenty, also."

"Kelly..." Dover said, warningly.

"What??"

"How many straights have you actually filled to-night?"

"Maybe," Fox said, holding his cards up, "one."

"I fold," Dover said. "Mr. Adams?"

"I'll just call you, Kelly," Clint said. "You make your straight?"

Fox made a face and said, "Nah. I paired sixes." He put them down.

"Three aces," Clint said, and raked in the pot...

TWO

oth Fox and Dover were better at talking than playing, allowing Clint to win back the money he'd lost
the night before at Faro and settle up with the saloon.
Even so, he'd heard enough about the Callum Parts &
Supply Company to want to pay it a visit.

*****

Like most other things in Celia Flats, the parts and
supply company was a pleasant surprise. It was run by
Edward Callum who was a jovial fellow a few years older
than Clint with a face covered in long, dark whiskers. He
more closely resembled a mountain man than any sort of
business owner, but he spoke of his place with pride and
an infectious enthusiasm.

"Y'ever done any smithing?" Edward had asked,
after the two men had introduced themselves to one
another. Edward sat relaxed behind his desk.

"Sure have. Mostly gun barrels and such," Clint
replied, downplaying his hand in that regard. He hadn't
bothered giving Callum his last name. Not yet, anyway.

"You been around mines much?"

"I have," Clint said. "Worked a few in California,
and around Eureka."

"Gold? Silver?"

"Yep, and other ore."

"Think you could forge parts for mining tools, cart wheels, or axe blades?"

"All at once?"

"If we're lucky," Callum replied with a chuckle. "I tend to get orders for all sorts of things, but this is the busy season. Don't know exactly what makes it that way, but it tends to be when I get most of my orders."

"Orders from where?"

"You name it. Anyone along the ol' waterway that needs something forged, I'll stoke the fires. Think you could handle work like that?"

Clint smiled at the prospect of spending some time breathing in the air blown in from the mountains and drinking some more of that Red Brew.

"I'm sure I could, Mr. Callum."

"Ed," Callum said,. "If you're gonna work here you can just call me Ed."

"Am I going to work here?"

"I think you are, Clint," Edward Callum said, "I think you are."

THREE

It was a warm day in the latter portion of summer. The season was far enough along for the heat to fade a bit although autumn was still just out of reach. Inside the small brick building where Clint was allowed to set up a workshop, the temperature rose with each passing minute that the forge was lit. By the end of the day, it was hot enough in there to cook a meal on the windowsill.

Clint was working on several long pieces of curved iron that was bound for a mine several miles north of town where they would be used as tracks for carts to haul ore up from the depths. It wasn't a difficult job, but one that needed special attention. The pieces were an unusual grade, which meant molds needed to be made and several first attempts needed to be tossed away to ensure exact measurements were maintained. After a full day of that, Clint was once again ready to put the saddle on Eclipse's back and ride to somewhere with a whole lot less people to please.

"Daddy!"

The feminine voice that came through the open window closest to where Clint was working was shrill and piercing. It was also familiar although he hadn't heard it raised quite so high before. Clint set down the tongs he'd used to dip his latest piece of work into a bucket of water and listened for a response.

7

"Shut the hell up," was the reply he'd gotten and it most definitely hadn't come from that woman's father.

"Ed!" Clint hollered toward the door that led into the next room. Last time he'd checked, Edward Callum had been in there working on a custom made sign for a gambling parlor upriver. When nobody answered him, Clint headed to the door to take a look for himself.

The next room was empty. A door on the far end was ajar as though someone had bolted through it in a hurry. Clint didn't like the look of that one bit and liked the sound of the woman's cry even less.

Callum's company consisted of three buildings. The largest was the brick one where most of the work was done. On the east side of that structure was a long narrow shed where supplies and finished products were stored. About ten yards south of that was a two room cabin with a sign that simply read OFFICE nailed to the front door. Once he'd stepped out of the brick building, Clint headed straight to the cabin, which was where the woman's shrill voice was coming from.

He quickened his pace when he heard heavy footsteps thump against the floorboards within the cabin followed by the rumble of furniture being knocked over. Upon reaching the cabin's door, Clint leaned his shoulder against it so he could enter without missing a beat.

"What the hell is this?" asked a tall, balding man with a long nose and sharp eyes.

The inside of the cabin was taken up mostly by two desks and several cabinets where ledgers, receipts, and any other sort of paperwork needed to keep the business afloat sat. One wall was dominated by a map of trade routes going as far south as Santa Fe and north all the way up into Wyoming. Sitting at the smallest desk was the owner's daughter, Sasha. Normally, she was a cheerful young woman who kept a smile on her face while balancing her father's accounts. At the moment, her blue eyes were filled with panic and her full lips were parted in a scream that hadn't been allowed to escape her.

There was another man in the cabin as well. He stood disturbingly close to Sasha with a large hunting knife gripped in a meaty hand. His features had the appeal of jagged lines that had been knocked into hard clay with a blunt chisel. The dark, thinning hair slicked down against his scalp didn't help him to look any better.

Clint saw all of this in the space of a heartbeat as his hand drifted toward the spot where a gun would normally hang at his side. The modified Colt wasn't there, however, since crafting riverboat parts and plow blades wasn't normally a dangerous trade. He'd taken it off and set it aside within easy reach, but had carelessly run from the building without it.

Surprised at first, the balding man quickly regained his composure once he saw that Clint was unarmed. "You ain't this one's daddy," he said.

"No, but I heard her scream," Clint replied. "You all right, Sasha?"

The young woman nodded silently. A few stray curls fell from the strawberry blonde hair that was tied back with a ribbon.

"Hey," the balding man snapped. "I was the one talkin' to you."

Ignoring him, Clint said, "Sasha, what's going on? Why did you call for your father?"

She took a breath in preparation to speak but before she could get a word out, the stout man beside her used the back of his hand to convince her otherwise. The slap sounded through the entire room. No matter how much

9

it hurt Sasha, Clint was going to make certain that big asshole would be hurt a lot worse.

FOUR

lint lunged across the room so quickly he could have been launched from a catapult. Both arms were extended so that when he reached the man who'd slapped Sasha, he could grab hold of him by the front of his shirt. He might have gotten some flesh in his grip as well, but that didn't keep Clint from pivoting his body and throwing the big man into Sasha's desk. Papers flew from the impact and the big man's legs were taken out from under him as he fell onto the desk and rolled all the way to the opposite end. By the time that one had fallen off to hit the floor, Clint had already turned his attention to the taller fellow with the balding head.

"You've got two seconds to explain yourself," Clint warned, guessing that was how much time it would take him to close the distance between himself and the other man.

"We ain't here to talk to you," the man said.

"You're here to slap a woman around? Is that what you want?"

"Our business ain't none of yours."

"I'm making it mine."

As he spoke, Clint hoped Edward Callum would respond to the sound of his daughter's voice. The owner of the supply company loved Sasha and was normally ready to take a swing at any young man who so much as

11

looked at her for too long. Now he was nowhere to be found. That worried Clint, but he didn't have time to fret about it and had just run out of time to stall. Now there were only two choices left: put up or shut up.

"Leave now," Clint said, "or I'll escort you out of here myself."

The balding man smirked and then spat out a snorting laugh. "You're half dressed and full of bean wind. Get the hell outta my sight before I tell Hobart here to pull your damn head off."

The squat man with the thinning hair, responding to the sound of his name like any obedient dog, pulled himself up and stalked forward in preparation for whatever his next order might be.

Slowly shifting his eyes between the other two men, Clint said, "Sasha, go on and get out of here."

"Sh...should I find Daddy?" she asked, sounding like a frightened girl half her age.

"Just go."

Hobart bared his teeth as if he was either going to yell at Sasha or bite her. He didn't get a chance to decide which because the moment he shifted his weight toward the petrified young woman, the big man was grabbed and spun away from her.

Clint took hold of Hobart by the arm and shoulder, pivoting to spin him in a tight circle before launching him toward the nearest window.

Because he was disoriented and forced completely off his balance, Hobart did all he could just to remain upright as he was launched across the room. It was a short trip to the window and since he didn't even begin to stop himself, Hobart smashed the glass and toppled outside.

Clint wheeled around to face the remaining man.

Even though it had been his idea to take Hobart for a dance, Clint wasn't immune to the dizzying effects of the sudden movement. Planting his feet a bit wider, he took a lower stance and locked his gaze on his target.

"So what the hell are you supposed to be?" the balding man asked. "That girl's sweetheart? That why you come charging in to her rescue?"

"I'm just someone who doesn't like to see animals like that friend of yours hit a woman."

"He does tend to get a little out of hand sometimes," the man admitted.

"Get the hell out," Clint said. "Or I'll get out of hand as well."

"How about I slap you around just like that bitch got slapped around before?" With that, the balding man took a swing at Clint.

Ducking under the punch, Clint snapped a few return blows into the other man's stomach. His fists thumped against tensed muscle without doing much in the way of damage. He was deceptively quick, even moving with the fluidity of a trained fighter. If not for the brush of sharpened steel against leather, Clint might not have even known something worse than another fist was coming his way.

The blade sliced through the air in a short, deadly arc meant to open Clint's belly like a gutted fish. Having heard the other man draw his knife from its scabbard, Clint jumped back and raised both hands high to let it pass. The edge of the blade raked against his torso, drawing some blood but not cutting very deep. He brought both arms down like hammers to pound into the other man's elbow. Not only did that force the knife down, but the man holding it was no longer able to maintain his grip on the weapon.

13

The blade was still clattering around on the floor when the balding man renewed his attack on Clint. First he took a few wild swings at head level. When those didn't land he followed up with some serious blows to the body. Clint weathered the few blows that landed, absorbing the solid knocks against his ribs while trying to twist around so the wind wasn't stolen from his lungs.

For the next few seconds, both men stood toe to toe while trading one punch after another. Clint could feel he was getting the advantage when more of his punches landed consecutively without being knocked away or interrupted by punches slamming back against his body. The balding man must have felt the way the fight was going as well because he covered up with both arms and took a few backwards steps from Clint. As soon as he had some distance, the other man reached for the pistol hanging at his side.

Clint didn't waste a moment before leaping forward. Using the same speed he might use to draw a gun if he'd had one, Clint slapped his hand down over the other man's weapon, trapping it in its holster before it could be skinned.

A wry little smirk showed up on the other man's face as he soaked in what had just happened. "That was sl—" was all he could get out before Clint's free hand balled into a fist and slammed into his face.

As the balding man stumbled back, Clint removed the pistol from his holster and flipped it around into a proper grip so the man was looking down the barrel of his own gun.

"Leave," Clint said. "Now."

"You gonna shoot me?" the other man asked while rubbing his jaw.

"Not if I don't have to."

"Then give me back my damn pistol."

Clint studied the other man carefully. There were several ways to tell if a man was going to pull a trigger, ranging from a facial shift all the way to how his feet were positioned. All of them were hints that the decision to take another person's life had just been made.

Even so, there simply wasn't any way in hell for one man to read another's mind without fault. For those times when he wasn't certain, Clint had to gamble.

Flipping open the pistol's cylinder, Clint warned, "I see you again and I'll just figure you've come back to do someone harm."

"That'd be a wise guess," the man said. "I can't imagine you'd even know who it is I mean to harm. That's my job and I do it damn well."

"Yeah," Clint replied while dumping the bullets from the pistol onto the floor. Now that the gun was empty, Clint tossed it back to its owner.

The balding man nodded after catching the weapon and then holstered it. "I'll be seein' you," he said while turning to leave.

FIVE

Clint stood at the office's broken window and watched the men leave. Once he was sure they were gone for the time being, he turned around to where Sasha was standing. "Are you all right?" he asked.

She stood as if her feet had been nailed to the floor, wrapped her arms around herself, and nodded.

Clint approached her, intending to have a look for himself if she was all right. Before he could check her for any wounds she might be too stunned to realize she had, Sasha wrapped her arms around him and held him tight. "I was so scared," she sobbed.

She wasn't cut or bleeding anywhere, which was all Clint had been looking for. Now that he had her so close, he could tell Sasha was more shaken up than anything else. Holding her at arm's length, he gently placed his hand beneath her chin so he could turn her head for a better look at her face where she'd been slapped.

"It's nothing," she said quickly and with a hint of embarrassment.

"Didn't look like nothing. Who were those men?"

"The big one was Hobart. The other was Jeremy."

"Jeremy who?" Clint asked.

"I don't know. My father only ever called him by that one name."

"Your father knows them?"

17

She nodded and pulled away from him so she could turn toward the window. Quickly, she was reminded of the damage done to that portion of the room and shook her head. "Daddy's going to be upset when he sees this."

Clint spun her around to face him. "To hell with that. How does your father know those men? Why were they here?"

"They work for someone named Stone," she reluctantly told him.

"You don't know any other name besides that, I take it?"

"Mister Stone," she offered.

"Come on, Sasha. You keep the books for this business. When it comes to accounts and other men that come and go through this office, I'd wager you know better than anyone what's going on. Don't play dumb now."

There was a definite fire inside the young lady and it flared up now. "I am not dumb," she said tersely. "And I do not play dumb. Not for you or anyone!"

"All right," Clint said. "Then don't treat me like I'm the dumb one. You know I'm right about what you know by sitting in this office day in and day out."

Those words were enough to defuse her temper, which left her pretty much where she'd been a few moments ago. Frightened and nervous, she started pacing the floor near her desk. "I do know most everything that goes through this office and I handle more of this business than even my father knows. When it comes to those two men and Mister Stone, your guess is as good as mine."

"I doubt that very much."

"You think I'm lying to you?"

"Not exactly," Clint said, "but I do think you can put more of the picture together than you're letting on. What did those men want from you?"

"They came in and tried to scare me. They were saying nasty things and making threats."

Since he could have put that much together on his own, Clint pressed her for more. Hesitant at first, Sasha finally told him, "I think this may have something to do with the Mescataine Company."

"Mesca...what?"

"It's no surprise that you haven't heard of them," she said. "They're a new company based in Nevada, I think."

"Those men work for them?"

"Maybe," Sasha replied with a tired shrug.

"Then maybe," Clint replied sternly, "you can find out for sure. I've got business of my own to sort out."

Suddenly, Sasha became anxious and she hurried up to Clint so she could put her hands on his shoulders. "Business? What sort of business? Are you going somewhere?"

"To find your father. It's strange that he hasn't showed up here after all the commotion."

Sasha's hands drifted down the front of Clint's bare chest. "You might want to put a shirt on while you're tending to your business."

"Yeah. I might want to do that."

SIX

hen Clint went to retrieve his shirt he also took the time to strap on his gun. After that, he went looking for Edward Callum.

It wasn't difficult to find the owner of Callum Parts & Supply. There were three buildings on Edward's property and Clint had already been in two of them. That only left the supply shed, which was Clint's first stop. Inside the shed, there was so much dust that a thick cloud was kicked up when Clint pulled open the door.

"Mister Callum?" he shouted. "You in here?"

"Yeah," came a grunted reply from the back of the cabin. "But I'm gonna need some help to get up."

Clint rushed inside, but not carelessly. Every step of the way, he was looking for anyone lying in wait for him and preparing for Hobart or anyone like him to spring some sort of ambush. The only living soul inside that shed apart from a small family of rats nesting in one corner was the man Clint had been hoping to find.

Edward was a bloody mess. His face was smeared with streaks of wet crimson and his clothes looked as though they'd been stored at the bottom of a hole before being slapped onto his body. When he stretched out a hand so he could be helped up, the wince on his face expressed the pain he felt all the way down to his toes in vivid detail.

"What the hell happened?" Clint asked as he lifted the older man to a standing position.

"I was gonna ask you the same thing. Think I was knocked out for a spell."

"How long?"

"If I knew that..."

"Right," Clint said. "Stupid question. Do you know who did this to you?"

Edward scratched his head. Even that seemed to hurt. "Damndest thing. I was in here getting some wood and nails to put together some crates, there was a pain in the small of my back and then...nothing."

"That's it?" Clint said, with a frown. "That's all you can remember?"

"For right now, pretty much."

"What about a fight?" Clint asked. "Did you hear someone coming? A voice? Anything at all?"

Edward shook his head.

"By the looks of you, there was some sort of scuffle," Clint pointed out. "Surely you recall something along those lines."

Looking down at his shirt, touching the side of his face, Edward looked as though he was examining a stranger he'd found lying beaten in a gutter. He continued shaking his head, but there was a great deal more frustration in the gesture.

"There had to have been something like that. Damn it to hell! I just can't remember."

Clint guided the older man to a stack of planks so both of them could use the pieces of wood as a low bench. "Can you recall anything at all? Other than what you already told me, I mean."

Edward rubbed his head before his hand drifted down to his brushy beard. "Why don't you tell me what

22

happened to you? Looks like you saw your share of a bad day."

"Not as much as you, but yeah," Clint said, before telling Edward the bare bones of what happened.

"Good God," Edward said, as he pulled himself up off the planks. "Is my little Sasha all right?"

"She's fine. A little shaken up, but fine. She can tell you everything herself."

Knowing that he wouldn't have been able to keep Edward still otherwise, Clint hadn't told him about the slap Sasha had received. Trying to get another word out of him after that would have been a lost cause and he needed just a few more words before cutting him loose.

"She mentioned someone by the name of Mister Stone," Clint continued. "That strike a chord with you?"

"No," Edward replied.

That was a lie and it showed up on his earnest face almost as well as an ink spot on a white cotton sheet.

"What about Hobart or Jeremy?" Clint asked.

Each of those names caused Edward's face to twitch as if he was still getting walloped by an unseen fist.

"I'll have to think about it, but...nothing jumps out at me."

"All right, then. Why don't you go see your daughter? She's in the office."

"She's all right?"

"Yeah. I just wish I could have done more to help her," Clint added.

"Like what?"

Clint had to take a moment to let that settle in. It had just been a very long time since someone had looked at him as something other than a dangerous man. He'd never lied to Edward about his years spent with a gun in his hand but the subject also hadn't come up and Edward simply took Clint at face value. Just another good worker.

"I shouldn't have given his gun back," Clint said, shaking his head.

"And that would have kept a man like that from doing harm?" Edward said. "There are plenty of other guns to be found. I'm sure he's probably got a few stashed somewhere real close."

"So do I."

"Every man has a gun to protect himself, Clint. And plenty of men carry them around wherever they go. But what sort of life is that? Always being afraid."

"It's not being afraid," Clint told him. "It's being careful."

"It's being ready to kill," Edward said. "Always ready to kill. That's not how things were supposed to be. This life ain't easy and this world can be a cruel place, but we don't need to walk around baring our teeth at everyone and carrying death on our hip."

"It's hard to argue with that," Clint agreed, "but those men are still out there and I'd rather not be unarmed when I see them again."

Edward sighed. "I suppose you're right." Touching his battered face and wincing, he added, "This has been a real shit pile of a day."

"Then maybe this isn't the best time I told you what happened to the window in your office."

SEVEN

dward's words still rang through Clint's head when he got back to his room at the Paddlewheel Hotel. More than anything, he wanted to take Edward's side and show he wasn't just another man carrying death on his hip. The truth of the matter was there was more to it, as it so often was. While he might agree with Edward's sentiment and even respect Callum for sticking to it, Clint just felt he was way too far down another path to change directions now.

It was a choice he'd made for himself a long time ago; one he'd been making again and again every time he chose to stand up to murderous bastards like the ones who'd slapped Sasha Callum in the face just to make a point. It wasn't a choice he was ashamed of, even for a second. It was just a shame that he'd had to make that choice at all.

This wasn't the first time such things had gone through his mind and Clint knew it wouldn't be the last. Once the familiar weight of the modified Colt was once again around his waist, his thoughts became clearer and he set aside anything other than the task at hand. First on his list of tasks was to check back with Edward Callum to make certain he hadn't had any more unwanted visitors.

Edward was in his office, comforting his daughter and cleaning up the big mess left behind from the scuffle with the two men. He was in good spirits, but didn't have much more to offer when Clint asked some more questions. Sasha was rattled, but feeling better as well, smiling at him almost every moment he was there.

Satisfied that they would be safe for a while, Clint moved on to his next stop. He hadn't had much need to call on the town's law since he'd been to Celia Flats. He knew the sheriff's office was at the corner of Longbow Street and Center Avenue. Despite the name of the second road, the office was situated near the southeastern corner of town. Not that it mattered, of course, since the door was locked and windows covered by drawn curtains.

Moving on, Clint headed up Longbow which was the main street through town. He kept an eye open for the sheriff who might be making the rounds, but didn't catch sight of anyone with a star pinned to his chest before reaching the Red Brew Saloon. Since he was there, Clint stepped inside and stood at the bar.

"Howdy there, Clint," the bartender, who also happened to be the owner, said. "Usual?"

"What time is it, George?" Clint asked. "Is it too early for a beer?"

"Never too early for one of my beers!"

"You sold me. I'll take one."

The mug was already half full before Clint had finished his sentence. As soon as the beer was in front of him, Clint picked up the mug and took a long pull of the rich brew. After wiping some of the froth from his upper lip, he said, "That tastes different than last time."

The barkeep leaned on one elbow and watched Clint with an amused expression. "How so?"

"Sweeter."

"Go on."

"More...cinnamon?"

26

George snapped his fingers and pointed excitedly across the bar. "You're the first one to guess it!"

"What's my prize?"

"That beer you're drinkin'. Care for another?"

Although he wasn't altogether wild about the new addition to the formula, Clint agreed. A bad Red Brew was still better than most good batches of other beers he'd tasted. As he set the next mug in front of Clint, the barkeep said, "You look like hell."

"That's not a great way to appeal to your customers, George."

"You got a free beer out of me," George said with half a wave of his hand. "I'd say your good will hasn't gotten sour just yet."

The barkeep had a point, but Clint didn't acknowledge it. Instead, he replied, "There was some trouble down at Callum's. Not that any law was around to help with it. Where is the sheriff, anyway?"

"Probably up working his claim in the mountains or gone fishing somewhere along the river."

"So, either in a mine nearly a day's ride from here or anywhere along the river?" Clint asked. "Is that the size of it?"

"That about covers it."

"Would've been easier to say you didn't know."

"Would it?" George asked.

Clint sighed. "You make one hell of a bartender. Talking with you for any amount of time is more than enough to drive a man to drink."

George smiled proudly.

Taking a stab in the dark, Clint asked, "Ever heard of someone named Mister Stone?"

"Sure," the bartender said. "The owner of the Mescataine Company?"

"Yes!"

"He brings me some of the more exotic ingredients I use for my brews when he comes through here," George said. "Also, he takes kegs of my beer to be sold up and down the river for some very nice profit. Don't tell Eddie Callum about that, though." The man lowered his voice. "He offered to do the same, but Stone gets me a better rate."

"Has this Stone fellow come here recently?" Clint asked him.

"Not in person," George said. "He never comes around himself. He's been sending his boys to collect my beer or drop off my payments lately. Why?"

Clint placed his hands on the edge of the bar as if he was about to uproot the entire wooden surface with one mighty pull. "What do his men look like?"

"One's a big bastard with stringy hair," George said, waving his hands, "and the other's taller with almost no hair at all."

"When was the last time you saw any of them?"

"Not too long ago," George replied. "Why? What's all the fuss?"

"I've got a proposition for you to earn some very easy money."

EIGHT

The Callums lived in a modest house within eyeshot of Edward's shop. There were a few others nearby, but they were far enough away to give the family plenty of room on either side. Celia Flats earned its name by being spread out in every direction like a mess of weeds scattered on a wide expanse of dusty acreage. So, unless a man stood locked in a closet or outhouse somewhere, he always felt like there was plenty of room.

As one of Edward's only workers for the time being, Clint had been to the Callum home several times. Mostly, for supper and the occasional breakfast before putting in a hard day's work. This time Clint came without an invitation and, judging by the bright smile on the face of the young woman who opened the door, he was more than welcome.

"Clint!" Sasha chirped. "So good to see you! Come in."

Stepping inside, Clint removed his hat and placed it on the rack next to the doorway. "I just wanted to come by and see how you're doing after this morning."

It was after dinner time and the house still smelled like roast beef and potatoes. A breeze blew in through several open windows, rustling the lavender curtains hanging on most of them. Despite the bruise on her cheek, Sasha looked just as fresh and clean as the air drifting in from the river. She turned her face self consciously so that the bruise didn't show as much and slipped some of her hair behind one ear.

"I'm fine," she said. "Just like all the other times you've asked."

"All right, then. I'll stop asking."

"Oh, don't be like that. It's nice that you're concerned. Makes me feel all safe and protected."

"Not safe enough to keep from—" Before he could take another step down that path, Clint was cut off by a soft hand place against his mouth.

"Don't," Sasha said quietly. "Just don't. I'm fine. It's over. Let's just move on."

"I hope it is over."

"Is that why you're here?" she asked, following Clint into the next room. "Because you think a raiding party will come crashing through the front window? Or would you prefer they go crashing out through the window?" she added with a smirk.

"Your father didn't seem too happy about that."

"He'll get over it."

"Where is he, by the way?" Clint asked.

"Where is he ever? Sitting at the desk in his office. If I'm not there, he usually is."

Clint swore under his breath as he turned toward the front door again. Almost immediately, his path was blocked by Sasha who appeared in a flurry of soft cotton skirts and even softer reddish blond hair. Placing a hand on his chest, she said, "Don't bother."

"Don't bother with what?" Clint grumbled.

"Going to the office to check on him. He can handle himself just fine. Did you know he's got two shotguns stashed over there?"

"Two shotguns in the office? That seems like a bit of

overkill."

"One in the office and another in the workshop."

"Too bad there wasn't one in the supply shed," Clint pointed out. "He could have used it."

"That's true."

"How is he, by the way?"

Some of Sasha's good humor darkened when she thought about her father's condition. "He's fine. Looks worse than it is. At least that's what he says. He's up and around, though, and seems like his old self. He's a tough old bird and this isn't the first time he's dealt with threats coming from the likes of those animals."

"It isn't?"

"He deals with shippers all the time," Sasha replied. "Some of them want better rates. Some are looking for schedules of when something valuable is coming in or out. Every so often, one of them comes around to try and scare him. Not always like it was today, but it's just a part of the business."

"I suppose so."

"Besides," she said as she ran her hands along Clint's chest. "Now that you stepped in to protect me, I doubt we'll see those two anytime soon."

"We can't count on that."

Sasha's hands moved lower. One touched the gun at Clint's hip and the other cupped the one between his legs. "I'm not worried. The way you stormed in to chase them off. The way you threw one out the window like a sack of bricks. It was all so exciting."

Her voice trembled slightly and her eyes widened as she looked up at him. Clint could feel heat from her body as her hand stroked him through his jeans until his penis began to stiffen.

"You sure your father won't be back soon?" he asked.

"Yes."

"Well then," Clint said as he swept her up to carry her toward the stairs, "let's see if we can take advantage of that time."

NINE

asha's room was at the end of a short, narrow hallway. Clint carried her up the stairs and nearly knocked over two small tables along the way as he received directions that were whispered into his ear. In between every few words, Sasha would bite Clint's earlobe or flick her tongue against his skin which made navigation in the confined space that much more difficult.

When they were close enough, she swung her leg to kick the door open so Clint could carry her inside. The room was decorated simply with a small bed covered by a thick quilt and even more tables holding vases of flowers on either side of a single window. Clint only cared about them until he'd avoided knocking any more tables over. Once Sasha had been placed on the bed, his attention was focused squarely on her.

The upper portion of her dress was laced together by a thick string that was tied at the top. Once Clint tugged on one end of that string, it opened the dress like a gift and allowed him to slip it down off her shoulders. She wriggled on the bed, making it easier for him to undress her until Sasha's body was exposed to him. Her breasts were firm and round, capped by little pink nipples that were already rigid with anticipation. She sucked in a quick breath when Clint placed his hands upon them and began to massage her tits while kissing her deeply. Before long she was tugging at his clothes as well, pulling at buttons and hastily unfastening buckles until his shirt was open and his jeans were loose around his hips.

"I want you," she whispered as she reached into his pants to find his rigid cock.

His clothes had formed a messy pile on the floor where they'd either been dropped or tossed aside. Clint grabbed hold of Sasha's dress and took it off of her, moving quickly to do the same to the white slip that clung to her supple body. Her skin was warm and smooth to the touch. As his hands drifted up and down her body, Clint could hear little gasps escaping from the back of Sasha's throat.

Kissing a line from her mouth down along her neck, Clint let his instinct and desire guide him to where he wanted to go next. Soon, his face was between her breasts and his tongue was teasing her nipples.

Sasha moaned softly and even giggled as Clint's mouth found different spots on her. She placed her hands on the back of his head, sifting her fingers through his hair and gently telling him to either stay put or move just a little bit one way or another.

When he kissed her flat stomach, Clint moved off the bed so he knelt on the floor and reached up to rub her hips as his mouth drifted lower.

"What are you doing?" she asked while spreading her legs.

Clint didn't say a word as he pulled her closer to the edge of the bed so he could kiss and lick her hip and inner thigh. As her legs opened wider, he was given a full view of the downy thatch of hair between them. Clint moved his fingers through the soft hair to find the tender pink lips of her damp pussy.

"Oh my god," she whispered.

Clint smiled and then gently licked her pussy.

Sasha arched her back while gripping her quilt with both hands. Digging her heels into Clint's back, she parted her knees as far as they could go, granting him even better access to the sensitive parts that he was so eager to taste. She closed her eyes and turned so her cheek was pressed against the bed, savoring every flick of Clint's tongue and every brush of his lips against hers.

He tasted her for several more minutes, licking her thighs when she needed a chance to catch her breath. Just when she started to relax, Clint pressed his lips against her once more and didn't stop until she was brought to a shuddering climax. Even then, he kept his tongue on her clit so she was thoroughly spent.

Still tasting her in his mouth, Clint stood up and climbed on top of her. Sasha scooted back onto the bed a little, but couldn't move too much because a good portion of her strength had been sapped. When she opened her eyes again, Clint was looking down at her.

"Ready?" he asked.

Although her features gave Sasha something of an innocent look, there wasn't a trace of innocence in her voice when she said, "Good lord, yes," and reached down to take his cock in her hand.

After guiding him inside of her, Sasha wrapped her arms and legs around Clint to hold him tight as he drove his hips forward. Both of them let out grateful sighs as Clint entered her. Once he'd buried his cock between her thighs, he opened his eyes and looked down to find Sasha smiling as though she was enjoying a particularly good dream. Clint eased out of her and pumped in once more, causing Sasha to grunt and writhe beneath him.

From there, he started to pick up his pace. Clint thrust into her with greater urgency, finding it tough to pull out since her legs were clenched so tightly around him. Their bodies entwined and they rolled on the bed, winding up with Sasha sitting astride him.

"Well now," she said mischievously, " and what have we here?"

Clint grabbed her hips in both hands while pushing up into her. Sasha drew a deep breath, leaning back and savoring the way he filled her. Reaching up, Clint cupped her breasts and ran her nipples against his palms while Sasha began to slowly rock back and forth on top of him.

It wasn't long before she found a good rhythm that brought a wide smile to her face. Riding him with powerful motions, she took every inch of his rigid cock inside of her before grinding her hips in a slow circle.

Clint enjoyed watching the change in her face as she drew closer to another orgasm. Sweat trickled between her breasts, running all the way down the front of her body, over her stomach, and down past her waist. By the time it reached the slick spot between her legs, Clint could feel a stirring inside him as well.

He gripped her hips once more and drove up into her. After a few powerful thrusts, a powerful climax pulsed through Clint's body.

"That's it," Sasha moaned. "Give it to me."

As he exploded into her he said, "Oh, it's all yours."

If there were any illusions of young Sasha's sexual innocence floating around in Clint's mind, they were long gone now.

TEN

Hours later, Clint still lay in Sasha's bed. Both of them barely fit on the narrow mattress, forcing him to lay with one leg hanging over the side and her to drape half of her body across his. It wasn't a bad situation by any stretch of the imagination. Clint would have gotten a peaceful night's sleep if not for the concern circling his mind like scraps of paper in a dust devil.

Earlier, he was concerned about Edward showing up and finding Clint with his daughter. While Callum didn't have much of a temper, it would have been uncomfortable to say the least. As even more time passed, Clint considered hopping out Sasha's window and jumping off the balcony before being discovered. It was something that a teenage kid might do, but still had some appeal when he thought about explaining himself to an irate father.

But Edward had yet to show up at his own home. When Clint got a look at a clock near Sasha's bed, he saw it was well past midnight.

That concerned Clint even more.

"Sasha," he said while gently shaking the naked woman sleeping on top of him. When she didn't stir, he shook her again a little harder.

"Mmm...what?" she groaned.

"Your father still isn't home."

"Good. Maybe you should go back to your hotel room now. Daddy can be so protective."

"I'm sure he can," Clint replied. "But does he usually stay out this late?"

"When there's work to be done." It took some effort, but she peeled her eyes open all the way to look at him. "What's wrong?" she asked with a good amount of drowsiness still in her voice. "Is something wrong?"

Clint climbed out from under her and started gathering his clothes and gun belt. "Probably not, but I'll check on him all the same."

"Should I be worried?"

"No. You should be careful. Do you have any more shotguns laying around this place?"

"Yes. Two."

"Two by two, huh?" Clint said with mild amusement.

Sasha showed him a little smirk. "Daddy likes his bible stories. Us being by the river always makes him talk about Noah and the flood. That's not what he meant with the guns, but..." She flinched, turned her head, and wiped at a tear that threatened to drip from one eye. "I don't want anything to happen to him."

"Neither do I." Having finished getting dressed, Clint pulled on his boots and buckled the Colt around his waist. "And I don't want anything happening to you, either," he said while checking the pistol to make sure it was loaded and in perfect working order. "You get one of those shotguns and stay somewhere safe. First sign of any trouble, any at all, I want you to run the other way."

"I can handle myself," she said in a firm voice. "I ain't scared."

"I'm sure you're not, but only as a last resort," he told her. "Got it?"

"Now you sound like my father."

"Good," Clint replied. "He's a smart man."

As he made his way out of the bedroom and down the stairs, Clint listened for any squeak in the floorboards or rustle in a shadow that might betray the presence of danger. He watched for any movement, anything at all, that didn't belong.

Clint stopped.

He hadn't heard anything.

Hadn't seen anything.

There was a feeling deep in his gut that told him to be still for a moment and when the stakes were high, Clint always listened to his gut.

Moving only as much as he absolutely needed to, Clint looked at the room below. He was almost halfway down the stairs with his hand poised above the rail nailed to the wall. One of the windows downstairs was partially exposed thanks to a curtain that was pulled back by a velvet cord. Through it, all Clint could see was unyielding darkness.

He thought back to the last time he'd been in that room. When he'd carried Sasha upstairs, everything had been pretty much the same. There had only been a bit of light cast by a pair of candles that had since burned all the way down. Apart from those little flames, it had only been some light from the outside that had illuminated the room.

Clint was just about to start walking down the stairs again when he recalled the way the light from outside had played across Sasha's face. It had only been a sliver of moonlight, but was enough to make some of her hair shimmer invitingly. Of course, he may have just been in a poetic frame of mind with her hands working their magic on him, but that sliver of light had been there all the same.

It wasn't there now which meant the moon had stopped glowing or something was blocking it. Clint narrowed his eyes and allowed them to finish getting acquainted with the darkness. One possibility was that a bank of clouds had simply drifted through the sky. Another was that the light was being blocked by something much closer.

Although he was quickly able to pick out more shapes in the sleeping house, Clint could only see a solid mass of black through the slim opening in the curtains on that window. It looked as though someone had completely covered the glass with black paint.

Just then, a gust of wind brushed against the west side of the house. A few loose shutters knocked against the wall. Some dry leaves scraped against another. Something stirred outside the window as well; something that was less than a few inches away from the glass.

Clint bolted down the stairs, drawing his Colt along the way. His first thought was that someone was standing against the wall and had been frozen in place like a deer after being spotted by a passing hunter. The black mass moved down and away from the window, allowing the scant bit of light to once again trickle inside.

Whoever it was, they were outside.

And they were on the move.

ELEVEN

Clint was out the door and circling the house in a matter of seconds. Unfortunately, that was enough time for whoever had been looking through the window to find somewhere else to hide. But Clint wasn't about to just let the peeping tom go. A field was directly behind the house on the same side as the window which was so open and flat that nothing larger than a squirrel could have hidden there.

That left three other sides of the house as possibilities. On his way out and around the structure, Clint had gotten a good look at the front and one side so he felt confident eliminating those. He reached his decision before his feet had come to a full stop, turned toward the north, and stalked forward.

Although his steps carried him in one direction only, Clint stretched out with his senses to cover every direction possible. He was just about to pick up his pace when he spotted a shape that didn't quite belong. It was a lump of dirt on the edge of the field behind the house. Since he'd written off that area as any place to hide, Clint had been ready to put it behind him. He'd also been ready to jump at the first hint of movement he might spot, which allowed him to stop right away to pivot on the balls of his feet.

The lump of dirt was about the size of a log that had

been covered in earth. If not for the dark soil contrasting with the lighter, dustier dirt surrounding it, he might have written it off a second time. But that lump didn't belong and that was enough to draw his full attention.

Clint considered shouting a warning to anyone who might be hiding behind the lump of soil. Whoever it was must have been sprawled on their belly or even partially dug in to the ground itself to keep from sticking out like a sore thumb. Since that put anyone at a disadvantage when it came to moving, Clint approached it without announcing himself.

He hadn't taken more than three steps before Clint saw the entire mound of dirt rise up from the ground like a body clawing its way from a freshly dug grave. The sight brought Clint to a stop as he dropped to one knee in preparation for whatever was to come next. Instead of attacking him directly, the filthy creature hunkered down and began running deeper into the barren field.

"Come back here!" Clint hollered as he pushed off with one foot to launch into a full run.

The thing didn't move very quickly. Once Clint caught up to it, he reached out with one hand to try and drag it down so he could get a better look at it. All he could see was a mess of black soil with leaves and a few small rocks stuck to it. The filth seemed to be covering a shape that was about the size and shape of a man, but before Clint could make out much more than that he was blinded by something that stank like the underside of a stump.

Whatever it was that was covering him was heavy and he was slowed down greatly by the weight that had just been added to him. When he reached up to feel what was clinging to his face and arms, he quickly realized that it had been dropped over his whole body like a sheet.

It didn't take long to pull off the dirty covering which held all the dirt, leaves, and small rocks he'd seen before.

"Nice try," he grunted, while tossing the dirty covering aside. "But you used up your trick. Let's see what else you've got."

The figure that Clint now saw was much different than before. Without the dirt and bulky cover he'd been wearing before, the other man proved to be skinny, agile, and quick as a whip. It was most definitely a man. Clint could see that much. Any more than that was impossible to say.

For a few seconds, Clint ran as fast as his legs would carry him. In that short amount of time, he became convinced that he wouldn't be able to beat the other man in a race. Not wanting to waste another second, he stopped, raised his gun hand, and took aim. Clint squeezed the Colt's trigger, sending a single shot into the night without causing his target to even stumble in the slightest.

"Shit," Clint snapped as he started running again. Whether the bullet had missed or the other man had simply made it outside of the Colt's range didn't matter. The skinny man was still running and Clint swore to himself that he would catch him.

Clint pumped his arms like the pistons of a steam engine, dropping the Colt into its holster within a few strokes. His boots pounded against the packed dirt and his heart slammed against the inside of his chest. All of those sounds melted into a percussive symphony within his head as his mind raced to come up with a way to close the distance between himself and his target.

With that much open ground, the other man would either need a secret hidden spot to hide or something else prepared as a getaway. Picking the latter as the most likely, Clint looked for what could possibly be the peeping tom's destination. He spotted a horse tied to a tree about fifty yards to the left and hoped he'd made a good choice when he veered off toward one of Callum's neighbors.

Clint ran full out, doing his best to avoid any bumps or divots in the ground that might trip him up. When he got to the house, he circled around it and headed back toward the horse he'd spotted earlier. If he was correct in his guess, he would have made the dark figure think he'd lost Clint along the way while Clint came right back around to catch him unaware. If Clint was wrong, the dark figure would have gotten clean away. It was a gamble, but since he obviously couldn't outrun the figure, Clint didn't have much choice. He simply had to hope his guess was right.

As soon as the animal came into view, Clint also spotted a figure crouching low and making his way to the horse. Although the dark figure was surprised that Clint had guessed where he'd been headed, he wasn't taken off his game for long.

It was hard for Clint to get a good feel for the size of the other man since the figure remained hunched over. Even when the figure turned to face Clint, he kept his shoulders at an odd angle and his arms spread out like a vulture walking on a desert floor.

It looked like the other man didn't intend on running any longer.

"Good," said Clint as he charged straight at him. "Let's see what you're made of."

TWELVE

The other man said nothing. The only sound he made was the rustle of his feet scraping against the ground and the subtle brush of a blade against leather. By the time Clint reached him, the dark figure was prepared to meet him and stepped aside to let Clint charge past him.

Having seen the knife in the other man's left hand, Clint twisted away before he was introduced to that blade up close and personal. As expected, the knife was swung at Clint's ribs. While Clint avoided that blade, he wasn't ready for the second one in the man's other hand. That one caught Clint's upper arm, slicing easily through the material of his shirt to open a gash in his flesh. Clint might have used his gun at that moment, but he wanted to keep the man alive to find out who he was, and who had sent him.

Snapping a fist into the other man's gut, Clint said, "Who are you?"

The man responded only with a quick swipe of a blade toward Clint's throat.

Clint leaned back, blocked an attempt to gut him by the man's second knife, and then brought his head straight forward to crack against the bridge of the attacker's nose. The blow landed with a solid thump, driving the dark figure back a few steps.

Now that he had a few seconds to collect himself,

Clint studied his opponent as best he could. The other man was lean and carried himself like a trained fighter. He circled Clint like a boxer while keeping low as if he could launch into a wrestling match at any moment. All the while, he kept both knives dancing around him, making it tough for Clint to gauge where they might be going next.

This man was a definite professional with a blade.

The other man's face, hands, and arms were coated in a black substance that made his skin look as if it was made of gritty oil. Beady eyes watched him carefully without giving away anything about what he might be planning. All of the hair had been scraped from his head, leaving irregular patches of stubble on his scalp.

"Exactly what do you want from all these people?" Clint asked.

The other man kept circling.

Keeping pace with him while making sure not to allow the other man to get out of sight, Clint reminded himself to be ready for an attack from other sides as well. There was no guarantee that this man was working alone.

Trying to stall for another moment or two, Clint said, "How about telling me your name?"

Whoever the man was, he wasn't about to play that game. Instead, he snapped a hand forward like a whip to throw the knife he held.

Clint stepped to the side and drew his Colt in a lightning fast motion. There was no more time to waste. Firing from the hip, Clint sent a round through the air that met the incoming blade amid a brief shower of sparks. As the sound of the gunshot ripped between them, Clint felt a sharp pain in his wrist. He'd been on the wrong side of a blade enough times to know when he'd been cut. Unfortunately, it was pure muscular reflex that caused him to let go of the Colt and allowed it to slip from his grasp and fall away.

Stooping down to retrieve the weapon, Clint was assaulted by a flurry of punches and kicks from the dark man. As the first barrage came in, he covered up using both arms to keep any of the solid blows from doing much damage.

At the first opportunity, Clint grabbed one of the incoming limbs and twisted his body to the side. Having managed to grab the dark man's left ankle, Clint took him off balance by dragging him around and slamming him to the dirt.

The dark man broke his fall using his arms and free leg and then propped himself up with both hands.

Clint stood up straight, maintaining a hold on the dark man's foot. Holding the man's lower body at his hip level and forcing him to angle his body downward with his head close to the ground put the man well off balance for the moment.

Clint said, "We can still talk like civilized folks, you know."

With a scratchy growl, the dark man brought his free leg up and around to kick Clint in the side of the head. The impact of the man's boot sent Clint staggering backward as blobs of light danced in his field of vision. The dark man was able to pull his trapped leg free and get back to his feet. As soon as he was upright again, the man bolted.

Clint blinked away the colors clouding his eyes and shook off the dizziness following a boot to the head. Using memory more than what he could see, Clint found his Colt and brought it up in time to answer any more attacks that might be coming his way.

But there was no target to be found.

Once again, the night was quiet and still.

The dark man couldn't have gone far, but he might as well have been swallowed up by the earth itself.

THIRTEEN

Clint barged into the office of Callum Parts and Supply with Sasha directly behind him.

"Ed!" he shouted. "You in here?"

For a moment, there was no reply. Clint was just about to turn and check the other two buildings when he heard a meek voice coming from a darkened corner. Instinctively, Clint tightened his grip on his Colt as he shifted his aim in that direction.

The voice was just a noise at first. When it came again, however, a few words could be deciphered. "Clint?" it said. "That you?"

"It's me, Ed," Clint answered now that he recognized the voice. "You all right?"

The owner of the place showed himself by standing up from the spot where he'd been cowering. "I'm getting real tired of being threatened on my own property."

"What happened?"

Sasha rushed past Clint to get to her father. Once she reached him, she hugged him tightly before stepping back to get a better look at him.

Clint could recognize the wounded pride in the older man's voice when he told her, "I'm just fine, sweetheart. Just leave me be."

She must have heard the tone in her father's voice as well because Sasha didn't seem the least bit offended by his brusque manner.

Turning to Clint, Edward picked up the shotgun propped against the wall beside him and said, "There was someone coming around to threaten me."

"Skinny fellow?" Clint asked. "Dressed in dark clothes with a dirty face?"

"It was Hobart and that other one, Jeremy," Callum said with a frown. "They were dressed in dark clothes, all right, but ain't neither one of 'em could ever be mistaken for skinny and...what'd you say...wiry?"

"There was a third man," Clint said. "Wiry. Used knives mostly."

Looking at him as though he thought Clint might be losing a small portion of his mind, Edward asked, "You sure about that, Clint?"

Peeling up his shirt, Clint said, "Does this look like I'm sure?"

Both Edward and Sasha looked at the thin red line marking the spot where the dark man's knife had found Clint's side. Sasha gasped and Edward squinted down at the cut while asking, "And you're certain it wasn't one of them other two? After all, it was dark and all."

Clint pulled his shirt back down. "I'm sure. There's another man out there watching your home. Unless there's some other bit of business you haven't told me yet, I'm guessing he was sent by the same man who sent those others. Tell me more about this Mister Stone."

"He's the owner of the Mescataine Company, a fairly new outfit that works the river to run cargo," Callum explained. "Like most other businesses in these parts, his bread and butter is mining. Small operation, but he's growing at a pretty good rate."

"Probably not good enough for his liking, though," Clint said.

"You heard of him?" Edward asked.

"Not until coming to Celia Flats," Clint said, "but I've met plenty of others like him. Has he threatened you before, Ed?"

"Yeah, he has. He sends his two gun hands around every so often looking to acquire other men's claims, threatens to take 'em by force sometimes or just plain jumps claims outright," Edward explained. "He uses the same sort of tactics selling supplies. Wants to be the only one selling to the larger mining outfits and will do just about anything it takes to make it happen."

Clint was familiar with the cutthroat business that was gold mining, but allowed the older man to continue at his own pace. As Edward kept talking, Clint checked the office for anyone hiding in another shadow or lurking outside near one of the windows. His biggest concern was the window that had been broken earlier. That one was covered by a sheet and flapped against the frame with every breeze that snuck between the spots nailed in place.

"There's a way of doing things," Edward continued. "A way for a business like ours to grow and flourish. What Stone's doing," he said while shaking his head, "ain't that way. It's a disgrace."

"What happened to you here?" Clint asked. "You said those men came around to threaten you."

"It was the same story as before," Edward said dismissively. "Threats and rough tactics. Nothin' I can't handle."

Clint knew there was more and he was fairly certain why Edward Callum didn't want to talk about it. Touching the spot on his shirt that had been sliced open by the dark man's blade, Clint said, "Sasha, could you get me some water and a clean towel?"

Happy to have something to do so she could help, Sasha hurried out of the office to get some water from the pump. Clint remained close to the window so he could hear every one of her steps, but lowered his voice so it wouldn't carry beyond the room.

"Tell me what happened," Clint said. "And don't fret about bruised pride. You're not the only one that got knocked around here."

While he was grateful not to look weak in front of his daughter, Edward was still a man who was accustomed to handling his own affairs. "It was Hobart again," he said. "Jeremy was close, but I couldn't see him the entire time."

"Was it like the other times they came along?" Clint asked him.

"No. It was worse. They were ready to draw blood this time. I could see it in their eyes. It ain't never been like that before. Usually, it's all just a lot of tough talk and swagger. Hell, they ain't the first to come along and try to drum up more business by acting tough."

"How bad is it?"

Edward shook that question off with a backhanded wave. "Wasn't bad at all until Stone got too big for his britches. Them two men of his have been coming around acting like they got the run of the whole river and every town along its banks. They never brought my family into it before, though. This time, Hobart told me they were keeping an eye on my girl."

Edward's face darkened the way any man's would when thinking about a threat made to their kin.

"I get it, Ed. What else?"

"The way they said it, I knew they meant business. I told him to go to hell and got him all riled up so he wouldn't want nothing more than to put me in my place.

Thought I'd get their filthy minds off of my Sasha."

"Not a bad idea. Why didn't you come get me, Ed? I would've gladly helped."

"Because I been tending to my own affairs this long and I can keep doing it!" Edward declared while straightening up to his full height. "Besides, I knew you were with her and that was gonna be good enough until I finished dealing with them other two. I got my shotgun, picked out a good spot, and intended on teaching them a lesson when they came back."

"How long were they gone?" Clint asked.

"Couldn't have been more than a few minutes."

"Then most of this happened while I was tussling with that man in the black clothes. That means Hobart and Jeremy are still nearby."

"Or headed this way," Edward offered.

"Right," Clint said while checking that his Colt was fully loaded. "I think I'll have a word with them."

FOURTEEN

Less than an hour later, Hobart and Jeremy returned to the office of Callum Parts and Supply. When they got there, they were greeted by a welcoming committee of one.

"Where's the old man?" Hobart asked.

Clint got up from the chair in which he'd been sitting. "Don't worry about that. I'm here. Talk to me."

"Already spoke with you. There ain't anything you got to say that I want to hear."

"Is that a fact?" Clint asked. "There are a few things I want to hear."

Before Clint could get another word out, Hobart waved him off as if he was shooing away a pesky child. "Ain't got time for this bullshit."

"What about now?" Clint asked as he moved his hand closer to the gun at his side.

Like any man who earned his living by sending lead through the air, Hobart's hackles were raised when he saw another man reach for a pistol. His muscles tensed and he squared himself up to Clint while saying, "What the hell do you want?"

"What do you expect to gain by threatening a man's family?" Clint asked.

"We're just doing business, and it ain't none of yours," Hobart replied.

"It is now," Clint said. "I'm representing Mister Callum's interests."

"Are you now?" Hobart sneered.

"That's right."

"How far are you willing to represent them?"

"As far as they need to go," Clint replied.

"And when did the old man decide to hire you on?"

"When do you think?"

A sly smirk drifted across Hobart's face. It was the kind of expression meant to provoke the man in front of him. Despite all of Clint's experience in dealing with assholes like this one, the attempt almost worked.

"He told you about us coming round and talking to him," Hobart said.

"No. I think Edward could handle the likes of you. It's when you started frightening women that I thought I'd have a word with you."

"What the hell are you talking about?" Hobart asked, frowning.

"I'm talking about the other man who works for Stone," Clint replied. "The one with the dirty face and scrawny build. Oh, and the knives."

"Don't know what you mean."

Hobart wasn't lying. Clint could tell from the confused look on his face. "All right, then," Clint said. "What did you want to tell Mister Callum? Whatever you meant to say to him, you can say to me."

"He's to sign over any claim he has to his mine. He'll sign it over to Mister Stone and he'll do it right quick if he knows what's good for him."

"And if he doesn't?"

"He knows what happens then. Same thing that happened to Bob Little in that camp up north of here."

"What happened to Bob Little?" Clint asked.

56

Hobart looked at Jeremy and both men grinned before he answered.

"Killed right in front of his family and everyone else in that camp. Ain't nothing like that happens there anymore, though. You know why?" Hobart asked.

"Why?"

Hobart grinned like a man who knew the cards he was holding could beat anyone at the table. "Because nobody else up there at that mining camp is as stupid as Bob was. They did as they was told and everything's quiet up there now." He stepped up to Clint and added, "Now run along and fetch Callum. There's still business to conduct."

"You can conduct the business with me," Clint said. "I'm his partner."

That surprised Hobart.

"Since when?"

"Since he started getting trouble from the likes of you," Clint replied. "Tell Mister Stone that nothing can be done to sign over Callum's mining claims without the rest of his partners' signatures."

"How many more of you are there?" Hobart asked.

"Just me and two others and they're not here."

"Oh, for Chrissake!" Jeremy said. When he came toward Clint, he stopped well outside of arm's reach. "This is just a goddamn waste of time!"

Hobart stretched a hand back to keep his partner from taking another step. "Where are the others?" he asked Clint. "Callum's other partners."

"Don't worry. I can get word to them," Clint replied. "But not until you tell me about the skinny man with the dark clothes."

"I don't have to tell you shit!" Hobart snapped. "You should just be grateful that we're gonna let you walk out of here. Go back and tell Callum to wait for word from Stone. He tries anything we don't like, even thinks about sending word to the law, and we'll pull that sweet daughter of his apart right in front of him."

Anger rolled through Clint's body. Even though he kept it in check, something must have showed on his face because Hobart latched right onto it. "You don't like that, huh?" he sneered. "Well tough shit. You can watch too and then we'll make you scream like a little bitch when we're through with her. What? You think you're the only hired gun that tried to step up to us?"

"You two must get tossed through a lot of windows," Clint said. "Or maybe you just forgot about what happened the last time you overplayed your hand with me."

The smugness was still in Hobart's face, but the fire behind it had died down considerably. "Maybe we'll just tear you apart first if things don't get signed over real quick."

"You'd probably just have that skinny friend of yours do it since you don't have the guts," Clint snarled. "Or is he too busy peeking in through windows?"

"Keep talkin', asshole. The more you flap them gums, the better it'll be to watch you cook when we burn this place to the ground with you inside."

FIFTEEN

Dawn was quickly approaching and nobody inside the Callum house was anywhere close to sleeping. While the rest of the town quietly approached the first few moments of their day, Edward and Sasha hurried from one room to another on the house's second floor while Clint kept watch through a window.

Having just heard Clint explain what had happened between him and the two gunmen in the miner's office, Edward sighed fretfully and asked, "What, exactly, was the purpose of all that nonsense?"

"First of all," Clint replied, "I'm certain those two don't know a damn thing about that killer I found lurking outside this house."

"How can you be certain about that?"

"Because neither of those two looked anything other than confused when I brought it up and they don't have much of a reason to lie about it."

"They could just be acting," Sasha called out from her room.

"Then they're better actors than I've ever seen," Clint said. "No, Hobart enjoyed tossing threats around too much. If he knew about that man I caught outside, he would've jumped on the chance to brag about it."

"So who the hell is that skinny skulking dog?" Edward asked.

Clint thought he'd spotted someone in some of the bushes across from the house, but it turned out to be a cat scrounging for something to eat.

"That's what I intend to find out," Clint said.

"What about second?" Edward asked.

Without taking his eyes from the window, Clint asked, "What do you mean?"

"You said the first thing you found out was that third man ain't one of Stone's," Edward said. "That means there's a second thing, right?"

"I didn't say he's not one of Stone's. I just said those other two didn't know about him."

"That don't exactly make me feel better."

"Second," Clint said, "I rattled their cages."

After a few seconds, Edward looked up from the bag he was packing and said, "And?"

"And, that can often prove to be very useful."

"For a hired hand that's too lazy to pan for dust at a smelly bend in the creek, definitely," Edward said. "For a couple of polecats who carry guns and like to split skulls, I ain't so sure."

Clint pulled the curtain into place so it covered the entire window and crossed the room to the door. Along the way, he passed Edward, who tossed a jacket on top of his bag. Clint then crossed the hall to Sasha's room and took up a position at her window so he could look down at another portion of the street outside.

"Those two are used to being the ones who make folks nervous," he said. "Those kind don't take well to it when the tables are turned."

"And when those kind get nervous, shots tend to be fired," Edward said.

"Good lord," Sasha sighed as she sat down on the edge of her bed.

"They're going to pull back and figure out what to do next," Clint said confidently. "That gives us some time to get the two of you out of here."

"So you said when you came back from talking to them two in my office," Edward groused while stomping into his daughter's room. "If you've got everything under control and have learned so much with all your talking, then why are we running away with tails tucked between our legs?"

"You need to get somewhere safe," Clint said. "I won't be here to protect you all the time."

"And I don't need that from you or anyone else!" Edward exploded.

Sasha jumped to her feet and stood between the two men, with a hand on each of their chests.

"Clint's right," she said. "It's not safe. And before you shout some more, I know you don't need anyone for protection. You've been doing that just fine all my life. But he found that other man just outside this house and he could very likely be back."

"Then I'll handle it," Edward said while taking hold of his daughter. "I don't need to be told how to take care of my family or my business."

Although he turned away from the window so he could face the older man, Clint was careful not to put his back to the glass.

"I'm not telling you how to tend to your affairs, Ed. I was just trying to tell you what happened when I met with those men in your stead."

"And you've been doing that since you got back. You also insisted that we pack up some things so we can get out of here and until now I've been real patient while doing just that." Upon seeing a questioning raise of Clint's eyebrow, Edward shrugged and added, "Well, mostly patient."

"The important thing is that we keep your daughter safe," Clint said, which was mostly true.

"That's my job," the man said, "although I appreciate what you aim to do."

"Look, Ed. I've done a lot more in my years than dig in mines or work as a blacksmith."

"I know. You're also a gunman," Ed said.

"Where did you hear that?"

"Someone down at the Red Brew mentioned it. I thought it was just a story, but I've seen my share of gunmen to spot one after getting a few clues."

"I suppose so. What do you say?" Clint asked. "Will you let me check up on this Mister Stone?"

"How do you propose on doing that, exactly?"

"It seems he's sent those two men of his to make the same threats to some folks in that camp north of here as they made to you. I'll ride up there to find out what anyone else knows about them."

"What if they don't know anything?"

"Someone always knows something," Clint told him. "Even if it's just a few scraps here and there, I can put them together to get a clearer picture. At the very least, I can figure out which camps I should visit from there. I doubt Stone has his sights set only on this one."

"I should be doing this," Edward grumbled. "My business is the one at stake. Besides, I know plenty of folks in other camps around here. They'll be more willing to talk to me than to a stranger."

"That's true." Clint put his hand on the man's arm and lowered his voice. "So why don't you meet up with me after you've taken Sasha to your brother's place? You said it's just outside of Denver, right?"

"Yes."

"And you're certain she'll be safe there?"

"Stanley would die before letting anyone touch a hair on Sasha's head," Edward said confidently. "And he's also good friends with the sheriff out there. Denver's got a hell of a lot more deputies than we do, so she'll have plenty of guards with her."

"Good. After she's safe, meet me in that camp up north. If I have to move on from there, I'll leave word at the biggest hotel about where I'm headed. Just follow the trail until we meet up."

"It won't take me long," Edward said. "And don't worry. I can handle myself just fine."

"I'm counting on it."

SIXTEEN

The first train to Denver left at one o'clock that afternoon. Although it was no short ride to the station in Colorado Springs, Clint made sure that Edward and Sasha made it there on time and without incident. Even after arriving at the station to find it close to empty, Clint remained on his guard. The train pulled up to the platform and was loaded while he watched and waited.

There was nothing to see other than a bored conductor punching tickets and tossing bags to a tired porter on the passenger car.

"I don't like this," Sasha said as she stubbornly refused to climb onto the train.

"I know," Clint replied. "You told me as much ever since we left Celia Flats."

"But you still don't listen."

"I've listened," he said. "It's the obeying part that I won't do."

Showing him a lighthearted scowl, Sasha ran her fingers through Clint's hair and gave him a quick peck on the cheek. "You'd better come see me soon. And you'd damn sure better take care of yourself while you're gone."

"I will, on both counts."

"That's enough of the kissing and puppy dog eyes," Edward said gruffly as he nudged his daughter onto the train. To Clint, he said, "I still say I could be of better use if I stick close to you. After all, I haven't always been a businessman. I've had some experience in tracking too, you know. I could help hunt down Stone's boys."

"No need to hunt them down," Clint said. "After getting under their skin already and making it known I'll be headed to the other camp, they'll come to me."

"And if they don't?"

"Then that gives me more time to find Stone," Clint commented.

"Damn," Edward growled. "I wish I had more to tell you about where to find that jasper. All I ever got from him was a few threatening telegrams. On the few times I met him face to face, he came unannounced and didn't mention where he called home."

"You told me plenty," Clint said while placing a hand on the older man's shoulder. "Thanks to you, I've got more than enough information to start hunting him and his men down. Now, if you don't get Sasha someplace safe, I'll be distracted thinking about the two of you until I have to take you to Denver myself."

"All right, all right," Edward said, "You made yer point. We're going."

"Take care of yourself, Ed."

"And you save a piece of Stone for me. I'll come to join you before you know it."

"I'm sure you will."

There weren't many others boarding the train and the conductor shouted one last time for anyone else who wanted to hop on. Clint backed away and gave Sasha a wave when he saw her peek out from one of the grime covered windows of the passenger car.

The engine let out a few loud, steamy breaths before lurching forward along the tracks. Its whistle shouted its farewell to the station with a pair of shrieking cries as the train gathered momentum. Once it was safely away from the platform, Clint walked back to where he had left Eclipse standing with the reins grounded.

Clint wasted no time before climbing into his saddle. Pointing the stallion toward the trail leading away from the station, he snapped the reins and held on as Eclipse built up some momentum of his own.

"All right, boy," Clint said under his breath. "Time to see how smart I am."

SEVENTEEN

trictly speaking, it wasn't very far to Denver. As the crows flew, the trip was just over sixty miles. Unfortunately, there were some large obstructions that forced the tracks to wind in loops, circle around, and twist well off the straight and narrow path. Those inconveniently placed obstructions were called the Rocky Mountains.

"I hate this ride," Sasha said while pulling down the shade of her window.

"You've only been on it once before," her father said from the seat beside her.

"Yes and I felt like we were going to plummet to our deaths every second of it, just like I feel right now." Sasha glanced over to the old man and nine year old boy sitting across the aisle from them. The old man was asleep, but the boy stared at her with wide, terrified eyes.

"We're not going to plummet anywhere," she said to the petrified kid. "Don't you worry."

The boy looked away from her, but was still haunted by the image she'd put into his little racing imagination.

When she looked back to her father, Edward had a wide grin for her. "You never did get along with other children," he said. "Even when you were one."

"I still hate this ride," she huffed as she fidgeted in her seat.

"There ain't much more of it left. Just sit tight and

maybe rest yer eyes. That'll make it go by faster."

"You think I can sleep while on this train?"

"Wouldn't hurt to try," he offered hopefully.

The look she gave him didn't offer anything in the way of hope. Rather than continue trying to convince her to let her shoulders come down from around her ears, Edward leaned his head back and crossed his arms over his chest.

"Then at least keep quiet so I can maybe get some rest. You know how it is in Denver. All that noise and commotion makes it hard to have one clear thought."

She leaned her head against the window, allowing the constant rattle of the train against the rails to massage her entire body. Her eyes drifted shut and her breathing slowed before snapping right back inside of her again.

"Do I really have to stay with Uncle Stan?" she asked with a childish whine in her voice.

"He'll take good care of you."

"He smokes cigars. Actually, he never stops smoking them. It's disgusting."

"There are worse habits to have," Edward replied while nestling into his seat as if he was being rocked gently to sleep.

After a few moments went by, Sasha asked, "Can you tell me one?"

"One what?"

"One habit worse than those cigars. I swear they smell like they were buried in a swamp before being burnt and blown in every direction."

"He's your uncle," Edward said. "Be sure you treat him some respect."

"You know I'm respectful when I'm there with him," she argued. "But here and now, before we're in front of the man and his awful cigars, can you tell me one habit worse than those things?"

Edward drew a deep breath and shifted one last time before becoming still. Just when it seemed he'd dozed off, he grunted, "No. I can't. Happy?"

The train's wheels began to screech as brakes were applied to them. Outside the window, the rugged terrain moved past the passengers' bored eyes much slower than before.

"We're stopping," Sasha said.

Without stirring from his restful pose, Edward said, "Just to fill the coal supply, no doubt."

"I want to watch."

"You want to watch coal get dumped into an empty train car?"

"It might be water," she said with a shrug. "Either way, it's better than sitting in here thinking about those horrible cigars."

"And it's better than you squirming in your seat like a little girl. Actually, worse than that. I believe you used to be quite a good tempered girl. Now," Edward said as he looked over to the kid who'd been frightened by Sasha's words not too long ago, "I'd say most children have you beat."

The entire car trembled and the train finally ground to a halt. Before that happened, Sasha was already out of her seat and moving quickly toward the closest door leading outside. From the opposite direction, which was the front of the train, rusty metal squealed as a chute was moved into position above the car directly behind the engine. There was a slight rumble as fresh water was poured into a large tank to replenish the train's supply.

Sasha stepped onto the narrow iron grate bridging the gap between one passenger car and the next. She held on to a railing, closed her eyes and took a deep breath of cool mountain air. The water continued to pour, nearly drowning out the sound of something bigger landing on top of one of the other neighboring cars. She took no notice of the sound, lumping it in with the rest. She also took no notice of the footsteps knocking against the roof of that car, making their way to the balcony where she stood.

EIGHTEEN

She was standing with her arms crossed against the wind that rolled by when the door to the next car was suddenly opened. A slender man dressed in a dark blue suit stepped outside and looked Sasha up and down.

"Howdy," he said.

Nervously, she replied, "Hello."

"Headed to Denver or will you be staying on?"

She started to answer the simple question, but became uncomfortable being the target of the man's piercing gaze. "I've got a ways to go yet," she told him.

"Don't we all."

Although it had seemed like he'd had somewhere important to go when he'd stepped outside, the man made himself comfortable by resting some of his weight against the rail. He reached for his shirt pocket, opening his jacket just enough for Sasha to see the pistol strapped around his waist.

"I should be going," she said.

"So soon?" the man replied while pulling a cigarette case from his pocket. "But we just started to have a nice little chat."

"It's chilly. I should go."

Just as the man took half a step away from the railing, the train lurched into motion once again. Sasha had been reaching for the door handle, but the jerking movement of the train caused her to stagger back half a step. The man in the dark suit was close enough to keep her from falling.

Smirking as he caught her with one hand at the small of her back, the man made sure she was stable before saying, "Watch your step, honey."

A chill worked through Sasha's body, originating from the point where the man's hand was still pressed against the slope at the top of her buttocks. "I'm fine," she said. Even though she twisted away from him, she was unable to remove his hand from her body.

The man stepped back, running his hand along her hip and side before finally peeling it off of her. Using that same hand to tip his hat, he showed her a bald head and a serpent's smile. "Can't be too careful now."

"That's true, but I really should be going."

"Where are you going that's so important? We're all on the same train and can't get off it anytime soon. At least, not without some bumps and bruises."

Following his gaze toward the rail separating them from a nasty fall, Sasha moved once more toward the door leading into the passenger car. She was stopped when the same hand that had touched her before grabbed onto the latch that would have opened the way into the train.

"What's the hurry?" he asked.

"I want to go inside."

"But we're having a nice talk," he argued. "Don't be rude, now."

Putting on a flimsy smile, Sasha shifted on her feet. "I don't mean to be rude," she said. Since the closest door was blocked, she turned toward the door to the adjoining car. "Maybe we can talk inside."

"I like it out here."

Although the man wasn't reaching for his gun, his right hand was close enough to it to make Sasha nervous. Her anxiety grew when she tried to step past him and was immediately blocked by him stepping in front of her.

"Now I'm starting to get offended," he said as he grabbed her arm.

Before she could struggle against his grip, Sasha saw the door to the other car come open so a smaller fellow in dirty pants and a rumpled leather vest could step outside. She leaned over to look past the man in the dark suit and said, "Hello there! Could you hold that door open for me?"

The man in the vest didn't answer her. He merely stepped forward as if he intended on walking through both of the others in front of him. The man in the dark suit opened his mouth and let out a pained croak. His next breath was accompanied by a flow of blood that trickled over his bottom lip and down his chin.

NINETEEN

"**O**h my God," Sasha gasped.

The grip on her arm relaxed and when she pushed the man in the suit away, he stumbled and dropped to one knee while hacking to fill his lungs. Now, Sasha could see the handle of a large knife protruding from his back. The blade was in so deep that when the man twisted around to look up at her its tip was protruding from his chest and poking at the inside of his shirt.

"H—help me," the man croaked.

Sasha couldn't speak. She could hardly breathe. Her entire body felt numb and before she could shake it off, the man in the suit was hoisted up by his collar.

The man in the vest had a dirty face covered in enough scars to make him look like he'd been stitched together from rags of skin. He looked over to Sasha and studied her for a moment, which was enough time for the fellow who'd been stabbed to gather some strength.

"Help," the man in the suit wheezed again. "Get... help." As he said that, he reached down to the holster around his waist and drew the pistol inside. Because of the grievous wound he'd been given, the .38 was almost too heavy for him to lift. Pure survival instinct gave him what he needed to bring the pistol up and thumb back the hammer.

Glancing at the weapon, the man in the vest swatted it aside and slammed his victim against the closest door. He then swung the man in the suit like a rag doll, knocking him into Sasha before she could get away. She recoiled from the impact, stumbled over a loose board on the iron balcony, and nearly fell off the train as she fell toward the railing. Grabbing onto the thin iron barrier with both hands, Sasha stared down at the rocky terrain that was now moving faster past them.

The two men were in a struggle now that the man in the suit had found the strength to fight back. Still keeping his grip on the other man's collar, the one in the vest continued to slam him against the door. Sasha felt sickness fill her stomach when she realized the man in the vest was driving the knife deeper into the other man's back like he was pounding a nail into a thick piece of lumber.

Sasha could barely catch her breath. She'd seen fights before and had even seen a few men get shot in the street over the years, but nothing like this. The man in the vest had just stepped up without a word and ripped into the other fellow the way an animal tore into the soft flesh of its next meal.

After a few seconds of being frozen in place, Sasha's survival instinct kicked in. There wasn't enough space on the narrow balcony to get to either door, which meant escaping into one of the passenger cars wasn't going to be easy. Considering how handily the man in the vest was winning the fight, it wouldn't be long before he could turn his attention fully to his next target. Since the silent attacker matched Clint's description of the one who'd been lurking outside her window, she had a fairly good notion of who that next target was going to be.

Fortunately, the gun dropped by the man in the suit had clattered against the iron grate without falling over the side. Sasha picked it up and held it in her trembling hands. Perhaps knowing that the pistol was back in play, the man in the vest thumped his victim once more and let him drop.

"Don't come near me," Sasha warned.

The man's face was filthy. Dirt, old and new, mixed with what looked to be blood mixed with black grease. His eyes narrowed into slits and his body subtly shifted into a coiled stance.

"I'm warning you," she said.

Amid the rattle of the wheels against the track, the occasional blast of the train's whistle, the roaring wind, and all the other sounds that enveloped the moving lo-comotive, the man's silence was even more unnerving. Without a hint of fear in his eyes, he shook his head. Whether silently telling her not to pull her trigger or showing he was convinced she couldn't do it, he moved toward Sasha.

Every one of her muscles tensed, locking her in place even as her thoughts screamed within her head to do something. Do anything at all.

Shoot.

Run.

Anything!

But all she could do was stand where she was and watch him close in. By the time she was finally able to tighten her finger around the trigger, the silent man had already reached out to snatch the gun from her hand. He took it from Sasha with a brutal twist that sent sharp pain shooting up from her fingers and wrist. In the blink of an eye, the gun belonged to him and was being aimed at a spot between her eyes.

Sasha waited for the end to come. The man looked at her with a cold, cruel certainty that it would be upon her very soon. And then, something dropped down from above. It looked like a snake at first as it coiled around the killer's neck. The killer reacted by grabbing it and pulling to try and create some slack.

It was no snake, but a rope that led up to the top of the passenger car to her left. When the killer tugged the rope again, he dragged the man attached to the other end of that rope into sight.

Clint looked down at them from above, grinning like a cowboy who'd roped a prize calf. "All right," he said while hoisting the killer upward. "Let's see you get away from me this time."

TWENTY

Earlier

The plan was simple and the idea behind it was even simpler. Whoever the dark man that Clint had found outside of the Callum home was, he meant to do harm to either Edward or Sasha. If he wanted to hurt Clint, the situation would have already worked itself out one way or the other. The man was a predator and he would come after them again. Instead of hunting him down, Clint would just watch and wait for the man to make his move.

The thought of using another person as bait never sat well with Clint. This time, he wasn't doing that. The Callums weren't bait. They were targets and Clint believed he could protect them better if the man coming after them thought he had some sort of advantage. All he needed to do was convince the killer that his targets were in the open and then watch carefully for the next attack. If it never came, all the better.

As he thought through his plan while riding Eclipse along the narrow mountain pass, Clint thought it might actually be that he was using the Callums as bait. Unfortunately, whatever he called it, they were in danger and the longer they were hidden away, the more time that killer had to make plans of his own.

Clint snapped his reins, urging even more speed from

the Darley Arabian. Eclipse never needed a reason to put all of his steam into a powerful gallop and he carried Clint along the winding path with no hint of fear or reservation.

On one side of the trail, the terrain rose and fell in irregular rocky designs that would eventually rise into majestic, snow capped peaks. On the other side, slopes ranged from easy downgrades all the way to steep drop offs that could mean injury or worse for both horse and rider.

It was on the side with the drop off that gave Clint the best view of his target. Train tracks were situated where the ground was most level, winding between sharp rises and the occasional slope. Most of the time, Clint was able to keep pace with the locomotive that chugged along the iron path. He didn't mind when he had to allow the train to get ahead of him for a little ways, but allowing it to slip out of sight was unacceptable.

The original plan had been to board the train at its first stop or even jump on when he had a chance. That way, he could keep watch on the Callums from a safe distance. Less than a mile after the train had left the station where Sasha and Edward had boarded, however, Clint spotted a light gray mare with a skinny rider following it.

It had only taken a bit of scouting for Clint to be certain the rider was the very man he'd been after. Instead of boarding the train as a passenger or waiting for it at a station, the killer was taking a bolder path. Clint smirked and kept his eye on both the train and the killer until those two drew closer about eight miles later.

Once he saw the killer draw up closer to the back end of the train, Clint snapped his reins and steered Eclipse down toward the tracks.

Trusting the Darley Arabian to navigate the terrain

on his own, Clint watched the killer like a hawk. The other man caught up to the train, drew in close to the caboose, and swung a leg over his horse's back. Without a moment's hesitation, the killer leapt from his saddle and grabbed the iron railing surrounding the train's rear balcony.

The instant the killer's hands touched that train, Clint knew his time was limited. The other man had proven himself to be an efficient predator and wouldn't wait long before finding his targets and putting them down.

Rather than force the killer to move even faster by announcing his presence, Clint maintained the high ground for just a bit longer. There was something drawing near that could prove to be an even better way of boarding that train.

It took every bit of steam inside Eclipse's powerful body to overtake the train and eventually pass it by. All the while, Clint kept his eyes locked on the water tower about a quarter mile ahead.

"Thank God," he said under his breath when he heard the squeal of the train's brakes as it approached the tower. By the time the train drew to a stop beneath the tall structure, Clint was swinging down from his saddle.

"What do you want, Mister?" asked the kid with the dirty face who manned a chain that would open the tower's oversized spigot.

Clint grabbed the rope hanging from his saddle and hung it around one shoulder. "Just need to borrow your tower for a moment."

It was a quick stop to top off the train's water reserves and the young man tending the tower was busy doing his job. Anxious to maintain his schedule, the engineer tossed a wave to the tower and threw the levers that caused steam to pour from the pistons near the engine's wheels.

Now that his job was finished, the young man looked once more for the strange man who'd approached the tower. He found Clint climbing the narrow ladder leading to the top of the tower. "Hey!" the young man shouted. "Get down from there!"

"I intend to do just that," Clint replied.

The train whistled and started rolling away as Clint reached the top of the ladder and turned toward the locomotive. Hanging on with one hand on the ladder and one foot on a rung, he positioned himself so he was facing away from the tower.

"Hold on, Mister!" the young man shouted from below. "I'll help you down!"

"Don't bother," Clint replied before jumping from his perch.

"Jesus!" the young man hollered. His voice became swallowed up by the chugging engine, but Clint distinctly heard some unkind words including "crazy" and "bastard". Dropping onto the top of the train and falling flat on his face, Clint wasn't in a position to argue.

The last thing he heard the man yell was, "What about your horse?"

Clint hoped that Eclipse was taking care of that himself.

From there, Clint made his way toward the back of the train. His legs ached from the rough landing, but remained steady beneath him as he bounded from one car to another. He might have leapt straight over the gap between the next two passenger cars if not for a woman's scream that caught his attention.

Clint hunched low and held out both hands for balance while making his way to the edge of the car. There was a fight going on between the two passenger carriers.

He could tell that much from the clatter of boots against iron grating and the sounds of pained grunting. The train was quickly building up to full speed when he looked down and saw two men fighting for their lives. Right away, Clint realized one of those men had already lost that fight and the other was the killer he'd been after. Sasha was on that balcony as well, which spurred Clint to make his move as quickly as possible. The trick was to do so without getting Sasha hurt in the process.

When he'd brought the rope along, Clint's intention had been to use it as a way to hang on to the train if things got rough. He uncoiled it from around his shoulder, shimmied closer to the edge of the roof on his belly, and used the rope instead as a handle to grab hold of the killer by his scrawny neck.

The surprise attack had taken the killer's attention away from Sasha for the moment. Before he could check to see if she was all right, Clint had his hands full just making certain he wasn't the killer's next victim.

TWENTY-ONE

"**G**otcha," Clint said through clenched teeth.

While that was most certainly true, the killer caught at the wrong end of Clint's rope wasn't about to concede the fight just yet. He held on to the rope encircling his neck, pulling on it to create just enough room for him to draw a few choppy breaths. As he was hauled upward, he kicked and thrashed with everything he had. Much to Clint's surprise, he had quite a bit.

"Shoot him!" Clint said.

Sasha stood rooted to the spot, watching Clint as though she was just about to leap into his arms.

"What?"

"The gun," Clint said. "There's a gun. Use it!"

All of the joy at having Clint show up from out of nowhere faded as the situation came rushing back in at her once more. When he'd reached up to grab at the rope, the killer dropped the gun he'd been aiming at Sasha. She looked down at the weapon, not at all anxious to pick it up after it had already been painfully taken from her not too long ago.

"I...I don't," she stammered. "I don't think I can..."

"Sure you can," Clint said while moving his head to avoid getting raked in the eyes by a wildly slashing hand. "It's right there, honey."

Sasha nodded and dropped to her knees to retrieve

the pistol. Almost immediately, the killer's thrashing legs came at her. She caught the side of one boot on her shoulder, but dropped to lay flat on the iron grate to avoid taking any real damage.

Despite dangling from the end of a rope several inches off the ground, the killer was clawing his way steadily to an advantage. One hand had found the edge of the roof and one foot had swung up onto it so he could pull himself up as well.

"I've got it!" Sasha said.

"Take a shot," Clint urged. "Just shoot!"

Taking quick aim, she squeezed the trigger and sent a round up toward both men. The piece of lead sparked off the upper edge of the passenger car and might have drawn blood if the intended target wasn't already up there and out of sight.

Clint maintained his grip on the rope, drawing it taut in an attempt to choke the killer. At the very least, he figured he could make the other man pass out to bring a quick end to the fight. But the killer's fingers were wrapped around the rope and no matter how deeply it cut into his flesh, he wasn't going to let go.

If the killer wouldn't be brought down easily, Clint figured he could take him down hard. Still using the rope as a handle, he brought the other man in while driving his knee upward. The blow landed on the killer's stomach, pounding against tensed muscle twice in a row. For a skinny man he was surprisingly muscular. Clint was going to hit him again when the killer swept his feet right out from under him.

For a second, Clint thought he was going over the side of the moving train. He may have done just that if he hadn't kept such a tight grip on the rope. His fall was clipped short as he was brought sharply to the train's roof where he landed with a jarring thump. Not only did he lose some of the breath from his lungs, but Clint also lost his hold on the rope. Before the killer could get away from him, he lashed out with one foot to smash the other man's knee.

The killer grunted slightly in pain, which was one of the few sounds Clint had ever heard from him. Even so, the other man barely seemed affected by the blow. He dropped down low, managed to pull the rope away from his neck, and wrapped it around his left hand.

"What do you want with these people?" Clint demanded. He had to steady himself on top of the rocking train to keep from falling off.

The killer merely tightened the rope until he'd formed a rough covering for his knuckles.

"What does Stone want with them, then?" Clint said. "I know he hired you and you're probably just following through on your contract. That's a good work ethic, but it could also get you killed."

Like a cornered animal, the killer crouched down with his legs prepared to spring.

Clint could feel the moment drawing closer when the man would launch himself at him. If Clint moved too slowly, he would only trigger an attack. If he waited for too long, he would just be attacked anyway. He didn't need to let more than a second tick by before his choice was made for him.

The killer lunged at the exact moment when the train swayed to one side. That way, when Clint went for his Colt, he was off balance just enough to keep from making a well aimed shot. On his worst day, though, Clint Adams's shot was better than most men at the height of their talent.

He squeezed his trigger, clipping the other man

somewhere along his right side. Clint couldn't see much more than that because the killer had reached him and was raining blow after blow down upon him.

The impact of every other punch had some extra sting to it thanks to the rope wrapped around the killer's hand. Flesh was shredded from Clint's cheek and neck until he slammed the side of his pistol against the other man's ribs. As soon as the killer pulled back, Clint swung his Colt at his head. The other man dropped and rolled away until he disappeared over the side of the roof.

Clint didn't get his hopes up that the man had fallen to his death and cautiously approached the edge with his Colt at the ready. Suddenly, from within the car directly beneath him, Clint heard a woman's scream. He tossed caution to the wind and looked over the edge for the other man. A gunshot exploded from inside the car to shatter a window and someone fell away from the side of the train.

The land sloped away from the tracks, making it somewhat easier for the person who'd fallen off the train to soften his landing by rolling as soon as he hit the ground. Clint would have expected at least a broken limb or two after that fall, but the man who came to a stop after his roll was healthy enough to climb to his feet. The killer must have been made of steel to survive that fall.

"Damn," Clint said when he saw for certain that it was the killer who'd left the train. "That son of a bitch isn't getting away!"

TWENTY-TWO

The son of a bitch got away.

Clint got down from the roof and onto the balcony in a matter of seconds but he still wasn't fast enough. All he could see of the killer was a shape in the distant grass that became smaller with every second.

"Stop the train!" he shouted while charging into the passenger car.

Everyone inside was already on their guard and many of them had guns in their hands. Sasha, who also had a gun in her hand, was the only one who didn't seem ready to put a bullet into Clint's hide.

"I already pulled the cord," she said.

Now that he'd taken a moment to stand still, Clint could feel the train slowing down. Before it came to a stop, he stepped outside again and leaned over the railing to get a look at the terrain they'd left behind. He couldn't see a trace of the killer, which didn't calm his nerves in the slightest. Clint jumped off the train, drew his Colt, and searched as best he could.

After a short amount of time, the only thing Clint spotted was Eclipse galloping to catch up to the train. He was relieved when the horse reached him. He checked the animal out and found him in good condition. It took some convincing to get the angry conductor to tell the engineer to wait, but eventually the Darley Arabian and

Clint were loaded onboard and the train started rolling again.

Once inside the passenger car, Clint dropped onto a seat and let out a long breath. Sasha sat down beside him and Edward took the seat directly across from them.

"You make the other passengers nervous," Sasha said to Clint in a voice that was normally used for passing secrets in church.

Clint looked around to find the few other passengers in the car with them were huddled together on the seats that were farthest from Clint's end of the car.

"Funny," he said. "A man was murdered and tossed over the side, his killer got away, and I'm the one that makes them nervous."

"You did jump onto the train while it was moving," Edward pointed out. "And for all they know, you're no better than that other fella."

"And what do you think about all of this?" Clint snapped at him.

Edward shrugged and looked chagrined. "I dunno. Just sayin', is all."

"So you straightened things out with the conductor?" Sasha asked. "He was very upset."

"I paid for a ticket along with an extra fee for damages," Clint said. "Although I wouldn't be surprised if some of that fee was just a bribe for their trouble."

"Wouldn't be a bad idea," Edward said. Quickly, he added, "Just sayin'."

"Yeah, you're right," Clint sighed.

"So, what happened?" Sasha asked while anxiously scooting to the edge of her seat.

"With what?"

"With what?" she asked incredulously. "That killer was on this train! You came out of nowhere and tossed him off! What do you mean, with what?"

Clint looked over to Edward who, in turn, looked away uncomfortably. "You didn't tell her?" Clint asked.

"Not exactly," Edward replied.

Sasha went from anxious to uncomfortable back to angry again in the space of a few seconds.

"Tell me what?" she asked.

Seeing that she was only going to get angrier the longer she was forced to wait, Clint replied, "I had a feeling that the killer would come after you again."

"That was my feeling too," Edward added. "Hell, it was obvious, wasn't it?"

Sasha remained quiet with her arms folded.

"I also thought there was a damn good chance that the killer was still spying on us," Clint continued. "I didn't see him lurking about after I chased him away the first time, but he seemed good enough at lurking to get close again without me seeing right away."

"So you two talked about us leaving and going somewhere safe just so that animal could hear you?" she asked.

"Yes," Clint said. "But I'd be watching over you the whole time."

"And you knew about this?" Sasha asked her father.

Edward shifted uncomfortably in his seat. "I was afraid you'd tip our hand. Also, you'd probably be frightened."

Sasha glared at her father, which said a whole lot more than whatever words were churning through her mind at the moment.

"I was going to jump onboard the train myself," Clint said. "Just as soon as it left the station when I wouldn't be seen."

"You'd just jump right on, huh?" Sasha said.

"Yes," Clint replied. "I've done it before. I wasn't going to leave you alone for very long at all, since it seemed that killer would come after you or your father at any moment. When it happened, I'd be there."

"So why weren't you here when he did come after me?" she asked.

"Because I spotted him riding alongside the train, trailing it from a distance. I figured he'd try to fire a shot at it or maybe try to stop it somewhere along the way, so I hung back and watched him. As soon as he decided to jump onboard, I did the same. He just did it quieter than me."

"You can say that again," Sasha grumbled. "Sounded like a load of rocks was dumped on us. So what now?"

Edward and Clint looked at each other before one of them spoke up.

"Truth be told," Clint said reluctantly, "the plan was supposed to end up with that killer either dead or captured, so..."

"So this isn't even the blind leading the blind," Sasha said angrily. "It's the stupid leading the blind and I can't even tell which is which!"

"Hey now, little girl," Edward snarled. "Get that tone out of your voice right now!"

Sasha stood up and stormed out the closest door. Although the clatter of wheels on rails was loud, it wasn't as loud as the slam of that door hitting the frame when she shut it behind her.

TWENTY-THREE

The next car was part sleeper and part saloon. Clint had his eyes set on the far end containing the bar and some small tables as he walked down the narrow hallway leading up to it. From the corner of one eye, he saw into a small compartment that had its door open. There was just a fold-down cot bolted to the wall and a distressed blonde sitting on it with her face in her hands.

Clint stepped inside and knocked on the door frame. "Mind if I join you?" he asked.

"Might as well. It seems I don't have any say in what happens to me anyway."

"You know that's not true," Clint said without taking the seat he'd been reluctantly offered. "Your father and I were just trying to protect you."

"Is that why I wasn't told about this plan of yours?" she demanded.

"That was your father's decision."

"You could have told me yourself," she said, pointing at him.

"I suppose you've got me there."

"But you probably just didn't want to tell me we were being used as bait."

"I wasn't using you as bait!" Before he could list all of the reasons he'd listed for himself why that wasn't the case, Clint held up his hands and said, "You're upset and you have every reason to be. You want me to leave?"

Sighing, she examined him and said, "Every time I see you, you're an absolute mess."

"That's because every time I'm about to see you," he explained, "someone comes along to try and beat the stuffing out of me."

That got a giggle out of her. Standing up, Sasha touched the places where Clint had been so recently cut or battered. "You're doing all of this for me?"

"Yep."

"Then it only seems fair," she said while reaching past him to close the compartment's door, "that I do something for you." From there, Sasha placed her hands on Clint's chest and dragged them along the front of his body while lowering herself to her knees in front of him.

Clint was surprised by the turn of events, but wasn't about to resist as she tugged at his belt and pulled his jeans down. Sasha took his penis in her hand, teasing its tip with her tongue and then licking it up and down like it was a stick of candy. In no time at all, he grew hard within her grasp. Once he was erect, she wrapped her lips around his cock and began sucking it.

Placing his hands on the back of her head, Clint leaned back against the door and savored the feel of her warm, wet mouth enveloping him. The more she worked her mouth on him, the hungrier Sasha was for more. Soon, her hands were moving up and down his hips, pulling him in closer as she took every inch of his rigid pole into her mouth.

Before it was too late, Clint reached down to help her to her feet. Neither of them said a word as Clint hiked up her skirts and pulled aside her undergarments so he could reach between her thighs to feel her pussy. She was dripping wet and shuddered slightly when his fingertips moved across her clit. When he lifted her up, Sasha hopped off her feet so she could wrap her legs around him. After a few seconds and a bit of wriggling, he was inside her again.

As his cock slid into her pussy, Clint let out a relieved sigh. She'd driven him almost to the brink in such a quick amount of time that every muscle in his body was aching for more. For a few seconds, they remained perfectly still just so they could savor the moment that he filled her. His erection grew harder and the lips of her pussy became wetter until neither one could wait for one more second.

Clint started moving in and out of her in a slow rhythm. Sasha's hands locked behind Clint's neck, holding her in place as he pumped between her legs. He cupped her tight ass in both hands, lifting her up so he could drive all the way into her. Once his cock was buried as far as it could go, he pushed just a bit more. That was enough to drive Sasha crazy and her entire body clenched around him.

She pressed her face against the side of Clint's neck, letting out a muffled groan as a powerful climax rolled through her from head to toe. When her trembling subsided, Clint started thrusting again.

When Sasha put her lips against Clint's ear, she spoke in a hushed, raspy voice. "Harder," she begged. "Fuck me harder, Clint."

Giving in to his most primal of urges, Clint pounded his cock into her again and again. He tightened his grip on her buttocks, feeling her hips writhe in his grasp. Sasha's nails dug into his back and she grunted her approval with every thrust.

Her shoulders knocked against the door of the compartment, creating a soft rhythmic beat that steadily became faster and more intense. Clint slowed down a bit as his pleasure built to its peak. He looked in her eyes as he exploded inside of her, both of them wanting to scream out loud but fighting the urge. The last thing either of them wanted was to create another scene for the rest of the passengers.

Now that they were still for a moment, Clint could hear voices coming from the other part of the car where drinks were being served. A mischievous little smirk appeared on Sasha's face as her hand slid down between her legs. Clint felt her fingers rubbing his shaft as well as the wet lips wrapped around it as Sasha massaged the spot where he entered her.

Her face took on a hungry expression as she continued to rub herself as well as him. She focused on the sensitive flesh of her clit which caused her breath to come in short, excited gasps. Even though he was spent, Clint grew hard again just by watching the intense pleasure building on Sasha's face.

She trembled again, held on to Clint's shoulder, and arched her back against the door. When she bit down on her lower lip, Clint knew she was in the grip of another orgasm. He could feel her body clenching around him and her hips starting to slowly grind as though she was urging him to start pumping into her yet again.

"You're gonna wear me out," he said while lowering her to her feet.

"Is that a problem?" Sasha asked with a tired smile.

"Not at all."

TWENTY-FOUR

The next time the train stopped was at a station. It wasn't much of a station, but there was a platform and a ticket counter, which was good enough for the railroad. Since he was able to leave without another incident well before reaching Denver, it was good enough for Clint as well. He walked down to the livery car, took Eclipse's reins, and led the Darley Arabian off the hissing locomotive.

"I wish you'd consider continuing on like you planned," Clint said to the two people trailing behind him.

"Which plan is that?" Sasha asked. "The one where my father and I are safe in Denver or the real plan you two kept to yourselves?"

"The first one," Clint replied.

"And why would we do that? The killer is still out there, isn't he?"

Edward already had his sights set on a barn next to the little station where he was told he could rent a horse. Rather than continue arguing with his daughter, he hurried over there to haggle on prices for transportation to their next destination. Clint wished he could join him.

"He is still out there," Clint said. "Although, it's possible he broke his neck in the fall from the train and is lying in some weeds somewhere."

Sasha looked at him in much the same way she might look at a dog wearing an Easter bonnet.

"Yeah," Clint admitted. "That's a long shot, but it would be nice."

"If you hadn't curled my toes back on that train," she said in a quieter voice, "you might not get away with this."

"And now?"

"I'll let you move on with what you were saying."

"Thank God."

"So he's still out there," she said.

"From what I saw of how well he handled himself and how easy he made the jump onto the train," Clint speculated, "my guess is that yes, he probably didn't break his neck when he jumped off."

"So, now what?"

"Well, you could always go to Denver like I was saying before."

"If that killer is still coming after us, we're safer with you, Clint. Isn't that obvious?"

Honestly, Clint was surprised that she felt that way. Considering the silent killer had escaped him twice and had nearly buried the Callums while Clint was watching over them, he wasn't sure they were safer with or without him. He didn't want to frighten Sasha, but he also didn't want to blow smoke by telling her everything was just fine.

"There's a lot that could still go wrong," he explained. "I still don't even know the man's name."

"When someone is trying to shoot you," Sasha said, "or stab you or strangle you or hurt you in any other way, does it really matter what his name is?"

"Maybe not," Clint said, "but knowing his name could make it easier to find him."

"But since we already know he's a killer," she continued, "wouldn't it be safe to assume he would lie about his name anyway?"

"Well, look at this. And here I was thinking it was going to be my job to comfort you," Clint mused. "Not the other way around."

"Well" she said, "I suppose even a man like you can be surprised."

And there were some surprises, Clint knew, that were better than others.

TWENTY-FIVE

The camp Clint had heard mentioned was north of Celia Flats. Denver was northwest from there and they hadn't ridden for too long on the train so that meant they'd only gone slightly out of their way if they wanted to get to that camp. Of course, Clint figured the diversion would have been more than worth the trouble if it meant taking that killer out of the picture. Since things didn't quite work out that way, he had to suffer through a bit of inconvenience.

"How do we know that killer won't take a shot at us at any moment?" Sasha asked.

Edward flicked the reins of the big white gelding he'd rented. "We don't."

"Then how is this better than going to Denver?"

"I wanted you to go to Denver, if you recall," Clint reminded her. "You decided not to."

"That was when I thought it was just a short ride to that camp."

"It was a short ride. From Celia Flats."

"Then perhaps I don't like this idea as much as I thought," she grumbled.

All right, Clint admitted to himself. Maybe he had to suffer through more than just a little inconvenience. "I'm going to scout ahead," he announced.

"You're leaving us alone?" Sasha whined.

"You were all fired up to go with us," Edward snapped at her. "What the hell did you expect?"

Sasha didn't have an answer for that one. Or, if she did, Clint had ridden too far ahead to hear it. Either way, he was grateful for some peace and quiet.

They might have made it to the camp after one long day's ride if they'd set out from Celia Flats. As it was, with the diversion of their short train ride, the three of them needed to make camp once the sun dipped beneath the mountains to the west. They were in a region of Colorado where the mountains seemed to be encroaching from all sides. Some of the jagged peaks were part of the Rockies and others were large outcroppings situated on their own. Clint didn't bother trying to figure which was which. All he cared about was getting high ground and keeping it so he could keep careful watch on the camp where the Callums were sleeping.

It was a long night, but the starry skies above and the shimmering mountains all around made it easy to bear. Clint didn't allow himself to drift off to sleep. Instead, he watched the flickering fire and kept an eye on any surrounding area where an ambush might be sprung.

So far, the killer didn't seem interested in striking from a distance. Even if he was hurt from being tossed off the train, he would most likely try to creep in close and finish the job he'd started. Clint had crossed paths with plenty of dangerous men and he knew they all had their preferences when it came to taking a life. The ones who fired a rifle from a distance preferred to lay low and watch folks scramble after the shot had been taken. The ones who liked to get their hands dirty wanted to see death up close and personal. They wanted to smell it, feel it slick on their hands, taste the fear that leaked from the dying.

But those weren't the only ones who developed a taste for something. All hunters got a taste for their prey once they'd locked horns and spilled each other's blood. Even though he didn't know this killer's name, he felt like he knew the other man well enough to track him down.

The killer wouldn't make his move tonight. Clint could feel it down to the chilled marrow in his bones. But the move would come and when it did, he'd be ready. And that meant not going to sleep.

TWENTY-SIX

The killer's fire wasn't much more than a sputtering ember mostly hidden by a little pile of wood. It provided some bit of warmth but no light. The killer didn't need light. He'd spent so much of his time in the dark that his eyes were more accustomed to it than to the harsh rays of the sun.

What little heat the fire had been giving off was meant for the slender blade that had been stuck at the base of the flame since it had been sparked to life. The killer removed the blade now, watching its dimly glowing tip as he brought it close to the flesh wound in his side. Without hesitation, he pressed the hot steel to his flesh and held it there until the wound was sealed. Smoke was still rising from his skin as he set to work on other minor injuries he'd collected throughout the eventful day.

There were several scrapes and cuts throughout his body which he inspected and then promptly forgot about. Others were wiped off with a rag. Some of the larger gashes on his legs and knees had been opened when he'd jumped off the train. Several chunks of wood and little rocks were wedged into his skin on impact to nag him throughout the rest of the day. Now, he used the tip of his blade to dig the bits and pieces from his body, casting them aside like the trash they were.

Smoke curled from spots where his hot blade met

tender flesh without bringing so much as a twitch to the killer's face. Once he was done plucking the larger splinters from himself, he pulled his clothes back on and reached for the saddlebag beside him. Since he'd stolen the bag as well as the horse carrying it a mile or two away from the train tracks earlier that day, he didn't know what was inside.

First he found some strips of jerked venison, which he immediately started to gnaw. There were some extra shells for the rifle hanging from the saddle's boot along with a few dirty shirts. At the very bottom of the saddlebag was a tarnished locket on a chain. The killer dug it out, flipped it open, and found a picture of a young woman with her hair tied up with ribbons on top of her head.

Most likely, the smile on that woman's face was meant for the previous owner of the horse that had been stolen. It was meant for the man that had been cut up and tossed aside like all the other refuse that the killer no longer needed. She was pretty. Her smile was wide and seemed earnest. The killer looked at her for a few more seconds, feeling nothing.

Any memory that was dredged to the surface was quickly shoved back down.

Any flicker of emotion caused by thoughts of women he'd known and smiles he'd seen was casually snuffed.

The killer turned the locket over in his hand, placed it between his teeth, and bit down on it. He saw impressions had been left behind, which meant the locket was probably crafted from gold. It was worth something. The picture was not. The latter was removed and tossed into the flames before the former was snapped shut and tucked into the killer's pocket.

He flexed his arms, worked a kink from his neck,

and patted his legs. Any other wounds he might have acquired weren't serious enough to warrant his attention, so they were forgotten. That included the redness around his neck from the rope. The killer held his hands less than an inch from the faint light of the embers to soak up their last bit of warmth. He then kicked dirt onto the fire until it was smothered.

For the rest of the night, the killer sat in his place with his eyes fixed on the spot where the fire had once been.

In his mind, he contemplated several different ways to find the people he needed to kill.

He thought of several ways to kill them.

He slept some.

He thought some more.

TWENTY-SEVEN

It had been a rainy morning and the ground was a sloppy mess beneath the horses' hooves. Mist hung in pockets just a few inches above the trail, creating a thin gray curtain smeared by bushes on either side of the path leading into camp. Clint led the way down a winding road that eventually widened with carts and wagons parked along either side.

"Kind of a mess," Sasha said. "Just like any other mining camp I've ever seen."

"That's why it's a camp and not a town," Clint said. "What am I looking for, Ed?"

"Place called the Californian."

"Sounds like a saloon," Clint said.

"Not quite," Edward replied. "It's a store. Everything from shovels to bedrolls is sold there. Since it's one of the few places in this camp that won't blow away with a stiff breeze, it's also what passes for a courthouse."

Clint looked around and saw plenty of other store-fronts that weren't nearly as stable. Mostly situated in tents and old wagons that probably couldn't roll ten feet downhill without falling over, the wares on display were fairly impressive. Anyone with some money in their pockets could stock up on guns, ammunition, horse feed, and even a few wet sticks of dynamite. Those weren't the only things for sale. Women of all shapes, sizes, color, and creed strolled up and down the crooked road, smiling and showing what they had to offer to anyone who seemed vaguely interested.

"I see why you came here so often," Sasha said to her father.

"Mind your manners, young lady," Edward said. "Your mother's been gone for some time. Even so, I don't take much to soiled doves."

"What about you, Clint?" she asked.

"This is my first time here," he said.

"You know what I mean!"

Clint smirked and kept riding.

The Californian wasn't hard to find. As Edward had mentioned, it was the only structure in camp that looked to be anything close to permanent. There may have been some solid frames elsewhere, but in the middle of the most activity to be found, The Californian was it.

Flanked on all sides by long tents filled with willing women, The Californian looked to be anything but a supply store. From what Clint could see, it had started off as a simple square structure roughly the size and shape of a house. Over time, additions had been tacked on like growths protruding from a mole. Most of those additions were framed in wood, but one or two were simple tents that had been nailed in place where another room might be. People came and went from the main front door as well as several openings in the tents that had either been built in or more recently opened with a wayward blade. It reminded Clint of Deadwood in the old days, before Hickok was killed.

"You do a lot of business here?" Clint asked.

Edward reined his horse to a stop alongside him. "It's been a while, but yeah. Greg Sanders buys most of the gold and silver dug out of the mines around here. He's a blowhard like any other buyer, but he's always got cash on hand and he gives even better credit to be put toward goods sold in his store."

"Yes," Sasha said, while nodding to one of the several scantily dressed working girls lounging in and near The Californian. "I imagine that's quite a popular arrangement—for all kinds of goods."

"If anyone knows about that miner that was killed," Edward continued, ignoring the icy attitude coming from his daughter, "it'd be Sanders. How about I go in first to say hello? Couldn't hurt to grease the wheels, so to speak."

"Why do the wheels need greasing?" Clint asked. "You're already an acquaintance and I'm sure these folks would like to know what happened to one of their own."

"Folks can get mighty skittish around here," Edward told him. "Especially when it comes to strangers. Also, I'd rather not have my girl walking into that place. She's likely to be harassed by some drunks."

"I can handle myself," Sasha said.

"You go on ahead, Ed," Clint said. "I'll keep an eye on her."

"I'm much obliged." And with that, Edward swung down from his saddle and walked into the Californian through the front door.

Once he was gone, Sasha said, "You just did that to get under my skin."

"Maybe a little," Clint said. "But if your father thinks things would go faster after he has a word with him, let him have his word. More than likely, he just wants a drink with his friend before asking all sorts of questions. It's been a long couple of days, after all."

Getting herself situated in the saddle now that she was the only one on the horse's back, Sasha huffed, "I suppose you're right."

"What's your problem?"

"Excuse me?"

"Ever since we got off that train," Clint said, "you've been in one hell of a bad mood."

"Isn't there plenty of reason for me to be cross?" she asked.

"Yes, but...you'd need to have been shot in the knee to be this cross."

She lowered her head, smiling like the young woman Clint knew from before. "I—I don't want my father to think I'm sweet on you."

"Well, aren't you?" Clint chided.

"I think he might already know."

"Well, I'm sure he has his suspicions. He probably suspects every man's motives when it comes to you."

"No. Not just that. I think he...already knows."

"I heard you the first time," Clint said.

Sasha leaned over so close to him that he thought she might just fall from her horse. She managed to stay on its back thanks to a firm grip on the saddle horn as she whispered, "I think he knows about what we did. You know?"

"Oh!" he said, raising his eyebrows. "And so that's why you've been in a mood?"

"Not exactly," she said with a pretty shrug. "I just thought that he wouldn't suspect anything if I wasn't so nice to you."

"And you say I'm the one with the bad plans?" Clint grumbled.

"I don't expect you to understand. It's different for daughters than sons." She gave him a sly smile. "I imagine your father gave you a big old pat on the back when you bedded your first woman."

114

Sensing that the conversation would only get stickier from there, Clint climbed down from his saddle and tied Eclipse to a hitching post. "I think I'm going to check on Ed."

"Should I come with you?"

"Just stay put and keep your eyes open," he told her. "If anyone comes along that you don't like, give a holler."

"Ok."

Clint walked to the front door of The Californian and poked his head inside. The first thing he noticed was that there was, indeed, a saloon in there. The second thing he saw was the round-faced fellow behind the bar holding a shotgun. Both barrels were pointed at Edward's chest.

"Oh! Howdy, Clint," Edward said. "Glad you decided to come inside."

TWENTY-EIGHT

The room was wide open and sectioned off only by arches of wood comprising the frame of the structure. Some of the space was taken up by a bar and tables, some was filled by shelves containing dry goods and tools, while the rest was a mix of both. At the back of the room was a row of flimsy doors and tent flaps leading to other rooms where working girls waited for their next customers.

Clint's primary concern at the moment was the bar at the front of the place. Several men sat at tables and stood at the bar, nursing their drinks without a shred of concern for the old timer being held at gunpoint.

"What's going on here?" Clint asked.

"None of your concern, friend," replied the man with the shotgun. He had a round face, rounded body, and a round ring of dark hair going around the back of his head. Now that Clint got a closer look at him, he could tell the man was much shorter than Edward. Most likely, he stood on a box or something similar so he could see over the bar.

"Greg Sanders," Edward said, "this is Clint Adams. Clint Adams, this here is Greg Sanders. Me and him are old friends. Ain't that right?"

"Friends?" Clint chuckled as he approached the bar. "Seems like a mighty loose definition of the word."

Sanders squinted past Edward. "Did you say Clint Adams?"

"He did," Clint replied while extending a friendly hand. "Pleased to meet you."

Clint had been hoping to shake the bartender's hand just so Sanders would let go of the shotgun. What he hadn't been expecting was an enthusiastic greeting that nearly brought the little man over the top of his bar.

"I've heard of you!" Sanders said as he placed the shotgun down. "You won those poker tournaments on the New Mexico circuit."

"I won a few games in New Mexico," Clint said, "but I don't know if it was on the circuit or not."

"Doesn't know if it was on the circuit?" Sanders said while pumping Clint's hand. "Listen to this man. All modesty. How many men beat some of the country's best gamblers and then ride out on a posse to kill one of the territory's most wanted horse thieves?"

"You did that, Clint?" Edward asked.

"Well, I'm not sure about the details."

Waving Clint off, Sanders continued, "He sent a few dangerous killers to hell and came back with enough time to take saloon girls up to his bed three at a time!"

Edward straightened the front of his shirt that still bore the imprint of the shotgun's barrel. "Oh. Well that sounds more like it."

"Hey!" Clint said, noticing the disapproving grimace on Edward's face that Sasha had most likely been fearing. Even though he wasn't out to impress the older man, Clint didn't like being put into a disparaging light so quickly.

"Some of that may have been true," he admitted, "but it got blown into something much bigger, just like any other wild rumor."

Sanders was all smiles as he placed a glass and bottle onto the bar. "I know all about rumors and I can smell bullshit from ten miles away. You, my friend, ain't bullshit. You're the real deal."

Clint nodded and accepted the drink that had just been poured for him. "Well, thank you. I think."

Laughing explosively as he slapped the bar with one pudgy hand, Sanders said, "You're more than welcome. You're a goddamned legend! A goddamned legend is here in my place, drinking my whiskey!"

Whiskey wasn't normally Clint's drink of choice, but he took a sip anyway since it seemed to be smoothing things over without any gunfire. It must have been the expensive stuff, because it put a smile on his face.

"That's good," he said while looking at the glass. "Smooth."

"Nothing but the best!" Sanders said.

Edward leaned against the bar with one elbow, grinning as though he'd been in on the good times from the beginning.

"See now?" he asked. "Everything's just fine once we all get together and be friendly."

"You're still on the hook with me, Ed," Sanders told him while jabbing a fat little finger in his direction. "You don't get off that easy—unless Mister Adams here can speak on your behalf."

Edward looked at him expectantly, putting Clint immediately on the spot. He tried to kill some time by taking another slow drink, but neither of the other two men were about to look away so soon.

Finally, Clint asked, "Speak up about what?"

"About the money this one owes me," Sanders replied.

"How much is it?"

"Fifty thousand dollars."

If there had been any more whiskey in Clint's mouth when he heard that figure, it would have been sprayed across the wall behind the bar.

TWENTY-NINE

Clint didn't feel comfortable leaving Sasha in the open for very long, so he stuck his head out to ask her to come into The Californian. She did so after tying up the rented horse and took a seat at one of the nearby tables. A woman with dark hair who was close to Sasha's age brought her some water and a sandwich. Since then, the two had struck up a conversation and were obviously swapping humorous stories about Clint, her father, or both. Either way, she was safe and sound and that was enough for Clint.

When he'd returned to the bar, there was another whiskey poured and waiting at the spot Clint had left behind. "I appreciate it," he told Sanders, "but I think I'd prefer a beer if you have it."

"Do I have it?" Sanders bellowed. "Best in the damn country!"

"Better than George's Red Brew?" Clint asked.

Sanders paused, furrowed his brow in concentration, and asked, "You've had that red brew?"

"Yep."

"That's some good stuff. All right, then, one of the best in the country!"

"I can respect a man who knows when he's beat," Clint said. "I'll take one."

"Coming right up!"

"I'll have one too," Edward said merrily.

The jovial expression that had been on Sanders's face disappeared in the blink of an eye. Casting half a glance in Ed's direction, he said, "You should count yourself lucky that you ain't drinkin' through another goddamn hole in your head, Ed."

"Now what's this about a fifty thousand dollar debt?" Clint asked. "What the hell did he do? Promise to buy this place from you?"

"He swore up and down that I'd get a share in a cluster of gold mines up in the mountains. When I heard they were producing, I thought the easy life was on its way." Narrowing his gaze like sunlight being focused to a burning point through a magnifying glass, he added, "Turns out my name wasn't on one of those fucking ownership papers."

Turning to Edward, Clint asked, "Did you cheat this man out of a claim?"

"I didn't think the mines were worth anything."

"Then why'd you sell 'em to me?" Sanders roared.

Turning toward Clint so he didn't have to look into the other man's angry little face, Edward explained, "I heard about these mines that were being sold in a lot. It was buy all of them or nothing, which meant the price was mighty high. I couldn't pull together what I needed on my own, so I went to some friends of mine."

"Who all turned you down," Sanders cut in. "Because they must know you better than I do."

Edward held up one hand as though the barkeep was jumping at him and needed to be pushed back. Considering how far over Sanders was leaning, he wasn't too far off the mark. "They just didn't have it, that's all. I came here for a drink, we talked about the mines, and Sanders said he wanted in."

"And?" Clint prodded.

"And I took his money, pooled it with mine, and went to make the deal. By the time I got to the clerk to make the purchase, I'd had plenty of time to think it over. You ever done any mining, Clint?"

"Some."

"Then you know it's a gamble," Edward said. "A gamble where you can lose a hell of a lot more than just your money. It can take years off your life, sweat from your brow, the wind from your sails..."

Letting out a snarling sigh, Sanders said, "What he's trying to tell you through all them words is that he never made the deal."

"I was getting to that!" In a more civil tone, he said to Clint, "I couldn't take that kind of risk with a friend's money. It's his livelihood. Mine too! If those mines didn't produce, we'd both be in a terrible fix."

"But they did produce," Sanders said. "And they produced big! If my name was on those ownership papers, I'd have at least fifty thousand dollars profit. At least!"

"They produced that much?" Clint asked.

Edward put his head in his hands as he replied, "They found a vein running through three of the four mines. The fourth one had a bit of silver in it as well."

"Fifty thousand," Sanders muttered. "Probably more'n that even after getting my investment back."

"That is a lot of money," Clint said. "A man who thinks he's owed that much might do a lot to claim it."

"Yer damn right he would!" Sanders said.

"Like maybe try to kill for it."

"That's r—" Stopping himself cold, Sanders blinked a few times and sputtered, "Hey. What? Kill?"

He became aware that everybody in the room was suddenly looking at him.

THIRTY

"**M**aybe you hired some men to come after him or maybe even his daughter," Clint said.

"Hold up, now. Any problem I've got with someone, I take it up with him to his face. I don't hire nobody else to do my dirty work."

"Well someone's been killing miners," Clint said. "And that someone is also real intent on killing Ed, here. Even took a shot or two at his daughter."

"I'd never do anything like that," Sanders assured him. "I've never even threatened to do anything like that."

"Do you know anyone who would?"

"That depends on who we're talking about. I mean, most everyone in this camp has locked horns with someone at one time or another. Lots of threats get passed around. Lots of men make good on them threats, too."

"What about Bob Little?" Edward asked. "Was anyone cross with him?"

"He was spending a lot of time talking with Abe Dreskind over the last few weeks. The two of them held court at that table right back there," Sanders said while nodding toward the back of the saloon portion of the wood-framed structure. "Got heated sometimes."

"How heated?"

"You know how it goes. Men come in, they get drunk,

they set their sights on the same lady and don't want to wait their turn, things get heated."

Thinking he might cash in on some of the fearsome reputation connected to him in Sanders's mind, Clint slammed his fist down on the bar and said, "Things might get heated if we don't get some straight talk from you."

Sanders held his hands out to his sides and waddled back a few steps like a flightless bird.

"I try to catch whatever I can as far as what goes on around here, Mister Adams" he said, "but I can't catch it all. Most of the squabbles I see are just like I said. Lots of loud nonsense about nothing in particular."

"Did they argue?" Clint asked. "Throw some punches? Fire any shots?"

"They argued," Sanders said. "But not too loudly. Some punches were thrown, but not by Bob. He wouldn't harm a spider if it was biting him."

"Who threw the punches, then?"

"Fella by the name of Hobart. There was also another named Teague. Calvin Teague. He was the calm in the storm whenever they started having words," the man explained, "but it looked like he might be the one holding Hobart's leash, if you know what I mean."

"I know what you mean," Clint said grimly. Looking over to the older man beside him, he asked, "What's the matter, Ed? Any of this sounding familiar?"

"I've heard that name before."

"Calvin Teague?"

"Yeah."

"When?" Clint asked, while leaning against the bar so he could keep a sharp eye on Edward as well as the rest of the saloon.

"When I was trying to collect money to purchase the deeds to those mines. He was one of the fellows I thought might be one of my partners. We even signed a contract saying we'd all go in together on the deal," Edward explained.

"All of who would go in on it?"

"Whoever I could find."

"You drew up the contract?"

"No," Edward replied. "And it didn't even mean anything because we never pulled together enough men or enough money to seal the deal anyway."

"Who wrote the contract, Ed?"

"Mister Stone."

Clint nodded and took the beer he'd been given. "Now we're getting somewhere."

THIRTY-ONE

There were plenty of places to eat in the camp, but only a few that had tables and a roof above them. Since he wanted to get away from The Californian for a bit and didn't want to have his dinner standing at a cart, Clint's options were limited. There was a Chinese place near the eastern edge of camp that cleaned shirts as well as served noodles. They wound up there mostly because they were all tired of looking for someplace better.

Sitting huddled around a round table in the corner of a shack, Clint, Sasha, and Edward started their meal with vigor. Their enthusiasm died down as soon as they took their first bite.

"Good lord," Edward said, dropping his silverware onto the plate with a loud clatter. "This is disgusting."

"Does anyone know what sort of meat this is?" Sasha asked as she held up a mostly cooked piece she'd speared with her fork at the bottom of her bowl.

"I wonder if this is a better laundry than a restaurant?" Clint mused. "All of the other customers I've seen come through here have been picking up bundles of clothes and staying away from the dinner special."

"I think my noodles were cooked in the same water that was used to wash that last fella's trousers," Edward groaned, frowning at his bowl.

Sasha made a face while still looking at the piece of

meat she'd found.

"And I don't think this is chicken," she said.

"Or beef," Ed said.

"Or pork," Clint added.

Still too hungry to give up his meal completely, Clint took a mouthful of his portion and tried to chew it up before he had a chance to taste it.

"Tell me about this contract you signed, Ed," he said, to get his mind off the taste.

"It really wasn't much of anything. Just a piece of paper meant to keep the people that agreed to help me from deserting if things got rough."

"Was it legal?"

"What's that matter?"

"You can't be that stupid," Clint said before he could think to stop himself.

Both of the Callums looked at him and then looked at each other. Sasha seemed ready to flip the table over if she got so much as a nod from her father. Edward, on the other hand, wasn't as anxious to defend himself.

"I didn't mean to call you stupid," Clint said. "I just mean that you must know well enough that a contract can mean a whole hell of a lot if it's drawn up properly."

"It was drawn up properly," Ed told him. "And it's probably legal. Mister Stone wouldn't have had it any other way."

"You were working with Stone?" Sasha asked.

"I went to him to ask for a loan so I could try to get them mines. I knew they'd produce! I knew it." Suddenly realizing he was talking loud enough to draw the attention of the bustling Chinese couple who kept busy washing clothes and stirring noodles, Ed lowered his voice to almost a whisper. "I did everything I could to gain ownership of them mines, but nothing ever came of it."

"They did produce, though," Clint pointed out. "Is that right?"

"Right. And since I didn't have enough pulled together to get a piece of 'em," Ed explained, "I didn't see any of the profits. You ask any miner in this camp," he went on, while sweeping an arm toward the door that led out to the crooked paths and leaning tents, "and they'll all have a bunch of stories to tell you about the big batch of gold that slipped through their fingers somehow. They've all gone through the same thing."

"All right," Clint agreed, "but this isn't about all of them."

"Well it's more than just me!"

"I know, Ed. Just take it easy."

Whether it was to help Clint or just ease her father's nerves, Sasha put a hand on his arm and said, "Don't get all riled up. We're going to fix this. First we need to get to the bottom of why those men want to kill us and then we can see about this contract or whatever it is."

"The two things are more than likely related," Clint observed.

Although Sasha seemed somewhat surprised by that, Edward wasn't.

"I can't think of why Stone would want to kill me, other than what I already told you," he said. "Stone's a claim jumping prick. Always has been."

"When he came to you to try and take what you own in Celia Flats, did he mention anything about this contract?" Clint asked.

"He might have."

"And why didn't you ever mention it before?" Clint demanded.

"Because that contract's only purpose was to form

some kind of a company among the men who got together with me to buy up those mines. But we never bought anything, so that contract ain't worth the paper it's written on. All he even said when he did come around most recently was that I should give up my claim in Celia Flats just like I gave up what I tried to do here."

"Did he have the contract with him?"

"Yeah, along with the papers he needed to get the mines I do own." Edward stared at a spot on the table in front of him as if he was willing it to burn. "He threw it in my face just to spite me. Said we could tie up all our loose ends and once I signed over my other mine, we'd be through."

"Maybe we could still do that," Sasha said hopefully.

Edward shook his head. "It don't work that way with men like him. They always want more and more . Stone's no different than any of the others I've had to deal with while panning for dust and digging in the mountains 'til my hands bled. They want more and they aim to get it by squeezing it out of folks like me."

"So if that old contract is so worthless," Clint asked, "why would Stone waste any time on it at all?"

"I don't pretend to know what goes on inside the head of a man like that," Edward grunted.

"Might do us some good to find out."

THIRTY-TWO

As the sun dipped below the horizon, the nameless camp became even more alive. Much like a jellyfish that had been washed into a puddle on the beach, the camp writhed and squirmed in ways that were both beautiful and disgusting. Deals were made, passions were stoked, and most of it happened at The Californian.

It was getting close to midnight when a man with a long face and even longer hair walked up to the bar. When he didn't get noticed right away, he started banging on the warped wooden surface with his fist.

"All right, all right," Sanders said as he walked along the raised platform he'd built behind the bar. "What the hell crawled up your...oh!" he said when he saw who it was. "How's it going, Abe? I was starting to think you didn't get my message."

"I got it," Abe Dreskind said. "Something about a man who's looking to buy some dynamite?"

"That's right. You still have those boxes from that mine that was abandoned?"

"Most of it. Who's looking to buy?"

"That guy right over there," Sanders replied while pointing to one of the tables against the back wall. "He may also be looking for some guns."

"You mean the fella with all them whores?"

"That's the one. He's been waiting for a while, playing some cards. Now that the girls have taken an interest, I'm not sure how much longer he'll want to be out here with us when he could be in another room with them. If you know what I mean, huh?"

Since a blind man could have interpreted the leering grin on Sanders's face, Dreskind simply said, "Yeah. I know what you mean. What did he say?"

"That he's looking to buy guns or dynamite. If it seems too risky for you," Sanders said, "I can point him in another direction."

Strangely enough, those words put Dreskind somewhat at ease. "You know his name?"

"Adams."

"Never heard of him," Dreskind said. "Can you speak on his behalf?"

"I can tell you he seems all right to me," Sanders said. "Figured you'd want first crack at him."

Letting out a bored sigh, Dreskind grunted, "Eh, what the hell."

"You make a deal, I get my finder's fee," Sanders said with a wink.

"Whatever."

As he crossed the crowded saloon, Dreskind nodded or waved to the familiar faces he saw. Most of the women had already shared his bed for a price and he looked them over extra hard, trying to narrow down which one he might take to bed later that evening. If he made enough money on this deal that Sanders had sent his way, he might be able to spring for two of them fine ladies. To hell with any goddamn finder's fee.

As he approached the stranger's table, Dreskind looked to the women gathered around the man who sat there. Two of them were the finest of the bunch working The Californian. The third was a close runner-up.

"I heard you're looking for me," Dreskind said. "Adams, are ya?"

"That's right," Clint replied. "Why don't you have a seat? The ladies were just leaving."

Although the women gathered around Clint didn't seem happy about the prospect of leaving him, they all did as they were told.

"How much dynamite you looking to buy?" Dreskind asked while watching one of the girl's backside.

"None," Clint replied.

"Guns then."

"Nope."

"I'm gonna punch that asshole Sanders in the face," Dreskind muttered.

"No," Clint said as he drew his pistol and set it on the table in front of him. "You're going to sit down and have a word with me."

THIRTY-THREE

Dreskind smirked and looked down at the gun as if it was a toy. "You know I could just take that and keep it for myself if I wanted to."

"Go ahead and try," Clint said. After a few quiet seconds, he shrugged and added, "It was mostly just to catch your attention."

"Well, good job. You got it." Dreskind pulled out a chair and sat down. "Now what? I take it you don't want to buy anything."

"Tell me what you know about Bob Little."

"He's dead."

"How about something else," Clint said wryly. "Like what killed him. Or who?"

"Hell if I know. I was supposed to meet him outside his favorite whorehouse to discuss a business matter."

"What matter? And before you say it's none of my business," Clint added, "just know I've already heard that one."

Dreskind leaned forward and placed one hand flat upon the table. "You don't scare me and neither does that gun. Fact is, I don't know who the fuck you are or why I should tell you a goddamn thing."

"I'm looking for the man who killed Bob Little," Clint explained, "because I think that same man might be trying to kill me."

Baring his front teeth in a slimy sneer, Dreskind asked, "What if I killed Bob?"

"Then I'll do to you what should be done to any other murderer," Clint replied in a voice that was colder than the shooting iron on the table and sharper than the knife in his boot.

"Well, I didn't kill him."

"I figured as much. In fact, I believe you had business with him and some other people that got cut short by Bob's demise. Help me find his killer and I might be able to help you."

"How?"

"I might be able to give you a chance to finish whatever deal you started with Bob in the first place."

"But he's dead."

"It was a mining deal, right?" Clint asked.

Warily, Dreskind replied, "Yeah."

"Is the mine still there?"

"Where would it go?"

"Exactly," Clint replied smartly.

Even though he was figuring this out as he went, he spoke with supreme confidence. Over the years, he found if he spoke with enough confidence, he might convince himself of his cause as he also convinced whoever was sitting in front of him at the time.

"This is a mining camp," Clint continued. "Nearly every deal around here has to do with either a mine or whatever comes out of it. I'd bet damn near everything I've got that Bob was killed over a mining deal. That's why those same killers are after me and my partners. You help me find that man and the deal is up for grabs again."

"And what's to keep you from grabbing for it?" Dreskind asked.

"If all I wanted was another mining deal, there are

easier ones to come by. I'm after this one man and he happens to be the one steering this deal. That man winds up dead and we both get what we want."

Dreskind rubbed his chin thoughtfully. Soon, a suspicious frown crawled onto his face. "I think you're completely full of shit."

"Sometimes, but not tonight."

"You don't even know what the deal really is," Dreskind commented. "Saying it was about a mine was just a blind stab in the dark."

"You got me there," Clint admitted. "Like I already told you, the deal doesn't interest me."

"Maybe it will if you find out how much money it's worth," the other man said.

"Then you can shoot me at that time."

"Or," Dreskind pointed out, "I could walk away now and save myself some grief."

Clint leaned back in his chair. "If you were set on making money without going through some grief, you're in the wrong camp."

"Trusting you is a hell of a gamble."

"So is chipping away at the belly of a mountain range hoping for a nugget of gold."

"Why did I know you'd say something like that?" Dreskind sighed.

"Because it's obviously the right answer."

After taking a few more seconds, Dreskind said, "I don't know much that could help you. I didn't kill Bob Little and I ain't the law, so I don't usually sniff around matters of that sort."

"But you must know something. Considering how much you've dealt with Bob and this whole affair, you've got to know more than I do." When he felt Dreskind was retreating back into his shell, Clint asked, "What about

Calvin Teague? Or the Mescataine Company?"

"Calvin Teague works with a fella by the name of Stone. That's about all I know."

"Are either of them in this camp?" Clint asked without giving away how interested he was in the answer.

"Calvin Teague is usually either here or working his claim."

"And Stone?"

"I've only seen him once," Dreskind said. "Dresses like a dandy and surrounds himself with hired guns."

"Sounds about right. Let's start with Teague. Where can I find him?"

"This camp's a goddamn mess of mud roads and ripped tents," Dreskind said. "Best if I take you there myself than try to describe it to you."

Clint stood up, "Sounds good to me. Let's go."

"Wait a minute," Dreskind said.

"For what?"

"All I've got on you is your last name," Dreskind said. "Before I throw in with you, I need to know who the hell you are."

"Okay then," Clint said. "My name is Adams, but it's Clint Adams."

Dreskind's eyes went wide.

"The Gunsmith?"

"That's right."

"Jesus," the other man said.

"It doesn't change anything," Clint said. "There's no reason for you to be scared."

Dreskind surprised Clint by grinning.

"I ain't scared," he said. "I'm kinda...tickled."

"Tickled?"

"Yeah," Dreskind said. "I never expected I'd ever be working with the Gunsmith."

"Does it make a difference?"

Dreskind stood up.

"Just makes me think we can probably handle whatever comes along...together."

"Does that include Stone?"

"Oh yeah," Dreskind said, "Stone, and whatever he throws at us."

"Then I guess we'd better get going."

"Sure thing," Dreskind said, "lead the way, Mr. Gunsmith."

THIRTY-FOUR

"So what kind of deal were you working on with Bob Little?" Clint asked as he walked with Dreskind through the winding muddy trails woven through the camp.

"There was supposed to be some sort of big strike just waiting to be discovered," Dreskind said in a tired voice. "You hear a lot of that kind of thing on any given day around here, though."

"You'd hear that sort of thing in any mining camp," Clint said.

"I suppose. But this was supposed to be huge. More importantly, it was supposed to be real. There was some sort of deal that had already been worked out and some legal mumbo jumbo or whatnot in the contract that would put this big strike up for grabs."

"But you don't believe that," Clint said.

Glancing sideways at him while continuing to walk, Dreskind asked, "What makes you think that?"

"Because you're telling me so much about it. Either you don't have much faith in it or my powers of persuasion are even greater than I thought."

Dreskind chuckled. "If it's like most of the stories of its kind, there ain't much to it. Also, with all the men winding up dead around here, it's looking to be more trouble than it's worth."

As they rounded a bend and cleared a row of carts, Clint and Dreskind found themselves in what looked to be the middle of the camp. People with dirty faces shoved past them on their way to get to even more carts nearby or to one of the tents that flapped in the cold mountain breeze. Not even the fresh air blown in from chilled streams could cleanse the stench of all that humanity jammed so close together.

"What can you tell me about Mister Stone?" Clint asked after they'd passed.

"He's rich and he's a prick."

"It's funny how often those two go together," Clint pointed out.

Dreskind laughed, which was a rough, haggard sound coming from the back of his throat. The laugh turned into a cough and soon the cough became strong enough to stop Dreskind from taking another step.

"You all right?" Clint asked.

Dreskind grabbed his side, frowned, and opened his mouth without being able to form a word. For a second, Clint thought the other man was drunk enough that he was still laughing at the off handed joke he'd made. But soon the look on Dreskind's face shifted into something that wasn't humorous in the least. It was deadly...

Placing a hand on Dreskind's back, Clint asked, "What's wrong? Are you choking?"

Dreskind pulled in a breath and winced. "Something hurts," he said. Raising the hand that he'd used to grab his side, Dreskind saw his fingers were coated in blood. "Aww, hell," he grunted.

Clint saw the blood as well and grabbed Dreskind's shoulder to keep him from falling over. "What the hell happened?" he asked.

But Dreskind was in no condition to answer. He

144

wasn't even in any condition to stand. Suddenly he was dead weight and it was all Clint could do to lead him to the closest empty space between carts before they blocked the steady flow of foot traffic coursing along the filthy pathway.

"Son of a bitch," Dreskind wheezed. "Can barely... catch my breath."

Clint knelt beside him, pulling open Dreskind's jacket to try and find where the blood was coming from. The shirt under that jacket was light yellow, making it all too easy to find the dark patch of crimson on his ribs. Holding the jacket open even further, Clint found a small cut that had been made in the leather, probably with the thinnest of blades.

"You've been stabbed," Clint said as if he could hardly believe it.

"Yeah," Dreskind replied. "I think I figured that much out already."

"When did this happen?"

"Must've been out h—"

Dreskind went limp. His eyes no longer blinked, but stared at the same spot where they'd been before. In a matter of seconds, they seemed to stare straight through that spot and into something that no one else could see. What escaped from his mouth wasn't a breath, but merely the contents of dead lungs expelled by seizing muscles.

He was dead.

So much for he and Clint being able to handle whatever came their way.

It was too late to do anything to help Dreskind, but Clint wasn't about to let the man's death go unanswered. He jumped to his feet, searching the milling crowd for any hint of where the killer might have gone. In his mind, he retraced their steps from The Californian.

Clint headed back along the route he and Dreskind had taken. One hand rested firmly on his Colt, ready to draw the weapon at any moment. The rest of his body was committed to the task of finding a target.

THIRTY-FIVE

lint returned to the hotel where the Callums were staying. It turned out that The Californian wasn't the only wooden structure in the camp after all, but the sprawling saloon was by far the largest. There were a few others scattered here and there, surrounded by so many tents that they were nearly engulfed by them. The sign posted in front of the place they'd chosen was partly shot away, leaving just enough of the word "hotel" to be legible.

Roughly the size of two cabins stacked on top of each other, the hotel had obviously been slapped together in a hurry. Every board creaked loudly beneath Clint's feet, threatening to give way as he hurried upstairs to the two rooms there. Fortunately, they'd both been available so he had one and the Callums had the other. Clint had barely cleared the topmost step when one of the doors was opened and Sasha poked her head outside.

"Clint? Where have you been?" she asked.

Approaching the door, he said, "I told you not to open that door unless you know for certain it's me."

"I heard you coming through the front door. This place is so full of holes I can hear most of what's going on through the whole camp."

By the time she'd finished saying that, Clint was in the room and shutting the door behind him. "You still need to be careful," he told her.

Sasha held up the little Colt New Line .32 that Clint normally used as a holdout. "I am."

"Good girl."

"Now where have you been?" she demanded. "You left hours ago!"

"The bartender at The Californian agreed to help me find one of the men who might know something about that miner that was killed," Clint said as he crossed the small room to look out the window. Outside, the camp was still alive and kicking as if there wasn't a fresh corpse laying on one of its many crooked streets.

"And what happened?" Sasha asked.

"I found him and it seemed like he'd be able to help find this Mister Stone I keep hearing about."

"Yes? Did you find him?"

"No. The man I was talking to was killed. Stabbed when he was walking right beside me."

"Oh no. Was it the same killer from the train?"

"I'm pretty sure."

"Didn't you see him?" she asked.

"No," Clint replied as his stomach twisted into a knot. "I didn't even see it happen. It just...did. But a blade was used—a very thin blade. Dreskind didn't even feel it go in."

"Is that possible?"

"If the blade is wielded by someone who knows what they're doing."

"Like the man from the train?"

"Exactly. After he was killed, I walked through this whole damn camp and couldn't find that son of a bitch. I would've kept looking, but wanted to come back here to make sure you and Ed were all right."

"We're fine, apart from all the infernal noise in this

camp," she said while nodding toward one of the cots situated against the wall.

Edward Callum was stretched out on that cot, his left arm and leg hanging over the side. The older man's entire body shook with a snore than sounded like it was part snarl and part gurgle.

"At least someone's getting some rest," Clint said.

"I don't think we're in any danger," she said softly. "At least, not right now."

"What makes you so sure?"

"Because this killer likes to attack and then run away. It's what he's done the whole time, isn't it?"

Although he couldn't fault her logic, Clint wasn't so quick to let down his guard.

"There's no telling what he'll do next," he said. "What he did tonight was bold. If he's getting bolder, then we can't be quick to write him off even for a moment."

"And we can't become skittish little mice hiding in a hole, either."

"Is that what you think I'm doing?"

"No, but you want to protect us," she said. "I appreciate that. But you need to rest also."

Clint shook his head. "I can't. That might be what this killer wants."

"Or maybe he wants to get us all running for so long that we get tired and jumpy," she suggested to him. "Then we'll get sloppy."

"That's a good point," he admitted.

"If there's one thing I've learned from watching my father work his fingers to the bone for days and weeks on end, it's that no good work gets done by a tired man."

"Your father is lucky to have you."

"Well he's sleeping," Sasha whispered. "And right now, I'd prefer if you did the same."

THIRTY-SIX

Clint's room was next door and a short walk from the only other room on the second floor—the room Ed was sharing with his daughter.

The cramped space felt more like a large attic and even after they'd stepped into the next room, Ed's snoring still rattled the wall separating them.

"I don't even know if I can get any sleep," Clint told her, shaking his head.

Pressing him down onto his cot, Sasha said, "So you'll try."

"I need to keep looking for that killer."

"He's hiding right now," she reminded him. "That's what he does."

"And if he isn't?"

"Then he'll come for us again," Sasha said while tugging at the strings closing the upper portion of her dress. "Whichever it is, you won't be any good to anyone if you're too tired to keep your eyes open."

"I doubt I could sleep now if I wanted to," he said, repeating himself.

Sasha peeled down the front of her dress to expose her pert, smooth breasts and hard nipples. "I figured as much. That's why I thought I could ease your mind a bit."

"Sasha, I don't think—"

She stopped him by placing her lips on his. After a short kiss, she whispered, "Don't think. Just let me take care of you. And," she added while slipping out of her dress, "try to be quiet."

That might be easier said than done. Sasha only wore her slip, but that didn't cover much since the upper portion had been pulled down and she gathered up the lower portion to give her legs better movement as she crawled on top of him. Her hands worked quickly to unbutton Clint's shirt and then take off his jeans and boots. By the time she had him undressed, he was hard and ready for her.

Sasha's hand wrapped around his cock, stroking him slowly while she settled on top of him. Smiling down at him, she rubbed her pussy up and down along his rigid shaft, teasing him with her warm, wet lips. Clint reached up to cup her breasts, massaging them as she ground herself against him. By the time she finally put him inside of her, it was impossible to say which of them was more grateful.

Clint leaned his head back against the pillow that was half stuffed with what felt like straw. But with the smooth, velvety embrace of Sasha's hot pussy gripping him tight, however, such a thing was hardly noticed. After taking him all the way inside, she sat up straight and reached up with both hands to run her fingers through her strawberry blonde hair. He eased his hands down to her hips, held them tight, and pumped up into her.

Sasha bit down on her lower lip, letting out a soft little moan as a tremor went through her body. He pumped into her a few more times, driving as far as he could go until Sasha's eyes snapped open and she fought to keep from crying out. Her nipples were hard and sensitive when he touched them again. Before he could move his hips again, she gathered up her legs so she could squat on top of him.

From that spot, Sasha could bounce up and down on top of him, riding him hard enough to make the cot creak beneath them. As she rode him, Sasha tossed her hair back and grunted like an animal as her nails dug into Clint's chest. Seeing her like that was more than enough to get Clint even harder. Now he was the one who had to keep himself from making too much noise as he held on to her hips and felt her muscles tense and close around him.

Sweat glistened on Sasha's body and when she slowed down it seemed she needed to catch her breath. Instead, she merely took a quick rest before grinding her hips against him. Her legs stretched out on either side of him, bringing her down a bit so she could prop herself up with both hands on either side of Clint's head. Now she took a slower pace, taking every inch of his cock inside of her and grinding her body so he could touch every tender spot within.

When Sasha slowed down even more, Clint took over. He grabbed her body and rolled her onto her back. She kept her eyes closed and smiled as if she was enjoying a dream while spreading her legs open wide so Clint could settle between them. Kneeling on the cot, Clint entered her once more and then took hold of her ankles so he could hold her feet up near his neck. Sasha locked her ankles around Clint's neck, pulling him in while stretching back to grip the cot along the edge that was closest to her head.

Clint ran his hands up close to her ankles and all the way down to the slope of her hips. All the while, he continued to pump in and out of her. At one point, one of his knees slipped off the edge of the cot. Clint stood up to regain his footing and when he reached for Sasha again, she'd rolled onto her belly and arched her rounded buttocks up into the air. Shaking his head, Clint took a moment to enjoy the view. He couldn't wait much longer than that before positioning himself behind her and entering Sasha from behind.

Sasha grabbed the edge of the flimsy mattress and pushed her face against the cot so she could moan without making too much noise. Clint glided in and out of her slick pussy, burying every inch of his cock in her with every thrust. To keep her in place, Clint held on to her hips and fucked her harder.

After driving into her again, Clint stayed put and ran his hands along the tight curve of her backside. He swore he could feel her entire body purring as he stroked the smooth skin of her buttocks. Just to mix things up a bit, he gave her rump a little smack which brought her head snapping around to glare at him over her shoulder.

He looked her in the eyes and started thrusting again, pumping between her thighs while placing his hands at the small of her back. Sasha watched him intently, her face showing him that another orgasm was quickly approaching. Unlike the first one that had been a ripple through her body, this one built into a wave that crashed through her. When it hit, Sasha arched her back and let out a shuddering groan directly into the blanket she'd grabbed.

Clint's grip on her tightened as his climax erupted from within. He thrust into her one last time and a few seconds later, barely had the strength to remain on his feet. Sated, he climbed onto the cot and stretched out with Sasha beside him.

He may not have slept very long, but Clint slept very well.

THIRTY-SEVEN

The next morning was a busy one not only for Clint, but for the rest of the camp as well. As Clint stepped out of the hotel, he saw grizzled men leading mules and driving carts toward the outskirts of camp, heading into the nearby mountains. Their mud caked faces were as tired as they were determined and every one of those red eyed gazes was set on a particular spot within the rocky terrain, where they would dig deep for their fortunes in gold or silver.

Clint had some digging to do as well, even though he hated to leave the Callums on their own. He simply couldn't do what needed to be done if he constantly had to be on the lookout for an attack that he may not see coming, anyway. In the end, he, Sasha, and Edward all decided the Callums were better off staying in their room with their backs to a wall and a gun in their hands. Grudgingly, Clint also had to admit that they'd been attacked more often when he was around than when he wasn't. Rather than try to figure out the method to a killer's madness, Clint set out to find the one man he knew to be somewhere in camp that fit into this mess and was still drawing breath. While plenty of folks knew Calvin Teague by name, they all had different stories on where he could be found. But somebody had to know.

Most of the people he asked told Clint that Teague

liked to frequent the camp's whores. If he was choosy about who shared his bed, Teague might have been a little easier to find. Instead, he apparently paid to be with any soiled dove that he could find. In a camp like this one, that was like telling a fisherman to start looking for the best trout somewhere in a body of water.

He spent the better part of the day going from tent to tent, cart to cart, asking the locals about Calvin Teague. Some had never heard of him. Some hated Teague with a passion. Others owed him money. Even more were owed money by him. But they all pointed Clint to a different spot in or around the camp where Teague paid for the company of a woman.

Even though there were more than enough whores in camp, there were also some who plied their trade just outside of it. For a few of those, Clint had to ride a mile or so out. When he got there, he was treated to more colorful stories and then steered in another direction.

It was just past dusk when he stumbled upon a tent that looked like one of the worst in the entire state of Colorado. The outside was mold covered around the edges and its roof was sagging low enough in the middle that water sloshed inside after being collected from an untold number of rainy seasons. When Clint stuck his head inside, however, he was surprised to find a plush little space with rugs on the floors, pillows stacked three high, and air that smelled like the sweetest thing in Clint's recent memory.

"Well, hello there, handsome," said a sultry brunette dressed in a flimsy blue nightgown covered by a see through robe of the same color. "Are you looking for some pleasant company?"

When the brunette got closer, Clint was introduced to a sweet scent that quickly made it to the top of his list.

"Yeah," he said while looking around the tent's dimly lit interior. "I heard a man by the name of Teague comes around here. I'm looking for him."

The brunette brushed her fingertips along Clint's chin, looking him in the eyes in a way that sent a nice little shiver all the way down to his boots. "If you want a man, you're in the wrong spot."

"Oh, uh, it's not like that. I need to have a word with him, that's all."

Now that his eyes had adjusted to the flickering light inside the tent, he could make out the shapes of bodies writhing under blankets, occasionally coming up for air before diving back under again.

"The man I'm after is Calvin Teague," Clint repeated. "You must have heard of him."

"Oh, yes. Then you're definitely in the wrong spot." Before Clint could get too discouraged, the exotic brunette added, "But you're close."

"I am?"

She nodded. "He works at the Mescataine Company."

Clint felt as if he'd just been knocked between the eyes. "The Mescataine Company is here?"

She nodded.

"In this camp?"

She nodded and smiled. "You're awfully jumpy, Mister. Are you sure you wouldn't like me to help you... unwind a little?"

"I'm plenty unwound as it is."

"I can tell," she chuckled.

"I just want to find Teague."

"Like I said before," she told him while extending a slender arm past Clint and out the door, "he does work for the Mescataine Company."

"And where exactly would I find the Mescataine

Company?" he asked.

The brunette smiled, put her hands on her hips, and licked her lips ever so slowly. She looked around the room, where shapes beneath blankets were still writhing and moaning together.

"You know," she said, running her hand down his chest and to his crotch, "I've never seen a man come into this tent and leave without sampling what we have to offer."

"Is that a fact?"

"It is." She closed her hand over the bulge in his trousers. "And I see you're interested. How about I have the girls line up—"

"I have a better idea," Clint said.

She took her hand away from his crotch and stepped back. The scent of her filled his nostrils and almost made him dizzy.

"We might be thinking along the same lines," she said with a smile.

"But not in here," Clint said.

"I have my own tent out back," she assured him.

He studied her. She was a beauty, of that there was no doubt, but he wasn't about to change a lifelong rule.

"But I don't intend to pay," he told her.

She grinned seductively and said, "I don't recall asking you for any money." She took his hand. "This way."

THIRTY-EIGHT

The brunette's tent out back was smaller, but as plushly appointed, if not moreso, as the large one. And it reeked of the woman's scent—except that the smell was too good to use the word "reek."

She turned to face him as they entered, discarded the flimsy robe so she was only clad in the nightgown. She was tall and leggy, with breasts perfectly round and firm, like overripe peaches. Through the fabric of the nightgown he could see that her brown nipples were hard with very wide aureole.

"Come kiss me," she invited.

"I thought whores didn't kiss."

She rewarded his comment with a throaty chuckle.

"You trying to get me mad so I'll throw you out and point to the Mescataine Company? Not going to happen. I have to keep my record intact."

"Your record?"

"No man has ever left my tent unsatisfied."

"I'd be satisfied if you told me where I could locate the Mescataine Company's headquarters.

"Not that kind of satisfaction," she said. She shrugged her shoulders so that her nightgown fell down around her ankles. "What's the matter, darling. You don't like me?"

"You're absolutely beautiful," Clint said, "but usually when I kiss a woman I know her name."

"Chloe," she said. "Chloe's my name. Now come here and kiss me. You're starting to make me wonder."

"About what?"

"About you," she said, "and what you're like."

"Well, my name is—"

"I don't want to know your name," she said, cutting him off.

He moved to her, took her into his arms, and kissed her. It was tentative at first, but then her mouth opened beneath his and the kiss became hungry, avid.

"Oh my," she said, breathlessly. "Let's get rid of these clothes and see what's really going on."

*****

When they were naked Chloe stopped him from taking her to the bed.

"What?"

"Right here," she said, sinking to her knees in front of him.

She took his hard cock into her mouth and sucked him, her mouth hot and wet. She made it last what seemed like a very long time, and when he exploded into her mouth he roared, his legs went weak.

Chloe stood up then, wiped the corners of her mouth with her thumb and forefinger, and smiled at him.

"Satisfied?" she asked.

"Uh, I thought we were—"

"No," she said. "That's my bed. I don't share it. I just wanted you to be satisfied."

He looked at her, her beautiful body, realized he wasn't going to get to experience it. Not without paying.

"Yes," he said. "I'm satisfied. But I'd be more satisfied—"

"I know," she said. "Get dressed, and I'll show you."

*****

Clint looked where she was pointing, trying not to be enticed by the smooth perfection of her skin or the enticing scent of her hair. It wasn't going to happen.

There were two tents larger than the others in the immediate area, only one of which appeared to be a saloon or opium den.

"That's the Mescataine Company?" he asked.

"You won't find any fancy offices around here, darlin'," she told him. Then she lowered her voice. "And just so you know, I don't think they take kindly to unwanted visitors. Especially at this hour."

"I don't think I'd be a wanted visitor at any hour," he assured her.

Eyeing him from head to toe and licking her lips, the brunette purred, "Oh, I doubt that."

Clint tipped his hat to her and walked away from the exotic brothel. As much as he wanted to look back at the fancy parlor of sin or at least take one more look at the lovely brunette who'd greeted him, he resisted. He'd been lucky to get away from there as quickly as he did. No need to push his resolve even further. The brunette had more animal magnetism than any whore he'd ever seen before. She might even have tempted his long time resolve to never pay for his pleasures.

There wasn't much of anything extraordinary about either of the two tents the brunette had pointed out. In fact, Clint had passed by them several times throughout the day. One of them was filled with small tables and— apparently—small stakes poker games. The other was covered by a flap that had folded down over itself.

Clint lifted the flap toward a hook on a post where it was meant to go. Once he'd fit the hook through a grommet in the flap, he could see a simple sign painted in black lettering that read: Mescataine Company.

"I'll be damned."

THIRTY-NINE

lint knocked on the tent's wooden frame, which shook the front portion of the entire structure. Roughly the size of a small cabin, the tent was one of the sturdier ones in the camp, which wasn't saying much.

"Come in," said a rich voice with a sharp tone that came from years spent in New York or one of the other northeastern states.

Stepping inside, Clint wore an easy expression on his face, while keeping one hand resting upon his holstered pistol. The man who'd called out to him to enter wore a plain gray suit and was seated in a simple wooden chair.

The interior of the tent was outfitted much like a Military commander's field barracks. There was a table in the middle, trunks and cases along the outer edge, and a cot situated next to a travel wardrobe.

The man himself had a slender build, sunken cheeks, and a pointed chin. His hair was thick, dark and wavy with subtle streaks of gray near both ears. And he wasn't alone. Standing equally spaced from each other on opposite sides of the tent, Hobart and Jeremy almost seemed like decoration instead of actual inhabitants.

"I was wondering when you'd finally step through that door, Mister Adams," the gentleman said.

Clint let out a short laugh. "So I'm supposed to believe you've been watching me that closely?"

"I didn't need to," the man said. "You've walked past my front door more times than I can count in the last two days alone."

"Guess you got me there," Clint admitted. "So you're the Mister Stone I've been hearing so much about?"

"Now I'm impressed."

"No, you're not," Clint said. "Since I've been asking around about you so much, you must've known about me for some time."

"Not as long as you might think."

"Long enough to try to kill me."

Stone walked across to a small cabinet near the spot where Jeremy was standing. By the time he got there, Jeremy had already opened the cabinet, removed a glass and bottle of whiskey and poured him a drink. Stone took the drink and held it up as if in a toast. "Would you like one?"

Smiling while locking eyes with Jeremy, Clint said, "Yeah, I would like one," just so he could watch the gunman fix it for him like a reluctant butler. Jeremy didn't disappoint and practically fumed for every second it took him to get a second glass and fill it.

To rub some salt into the wound to the gunman's pride, Clint stood his ground and made Jeremy walk to him to deliver the drink. "Thank you, my good man," Clint said.

If Jeremy was fuming before, he nearly caught on fire when he heard that.

Clint smiled, sniffed the whiskey, and set it down on the closest table.

"So, tell me, what brings you here, Mister Adams?" Stone asked.

"You should know."

"I honestly don't. I've been dealing with my own

affairs and suddenly you show up, a gunfighter of some repute if I'm to believe what I've been told."

"Dealing with your own affairs," Clint scoffed. "And that includes sending killers out to bring down innocent people when they're least expecting it."

Now it was Stone's turn to scoff. "Innocent? Hardly."

"I've met some of those people and I've seen your man try to stick a knife in their backs."

Stone shrugged. "Terrible things happen in this world. Surely you don't take it upon yourself to avenge every last one of them?"

"Your two men there are hired killers," Clint stated. "Men like me would come after them for a lot less."

"Are you a lawman?"

"No."

"Then why involve yourself in this?" Stone asked.

"Because you tried to have me killed along with those others I've talked about."

Clint had been trying to see if he could ruffle Stone's feathers in the slightest, but the dapper man in the expensive suit was having none of it. When he smiled at Clint, there wasn't a hint of sarcasm on his face.

There also wasn't an ounce of dishonesty in his voice when he said, "I never tried to harm you, Mister Adams. Pietro is the very best at what he does and the only reason you're drawing breath right now is because he was never actually told to kill you."

"Pietro, that's your blade man?" Clint asked. "You're that confident in him?"

"Oh, yes," Stone said. "I have the utmost confidence in him. If I had told Pietro I wanted you dead, you would have been dead a long time ago."

"is that a fact?"

Stone laughed and said, "Trust me."

FORTY

ietro sat in his room, which was only one of two on the first floor of his hotel. That is, if a cobbled together shack in the middle of a shit hole camp could be considered a hotel. While he noticed his surroundings, he wasn't bothered by them. He'd get whatever rest he needed wherever he needed to get it. Right now, he didn't need any rest.

The knife fit in his hand perfectly. It was balanced perfectly for his grip. Its blade was narrow enough to be hidden easily and drawn quickly, yet wide enough to do the job. It was light enough to be thrown and long enough to puncture something vital no matter where he decided to plant it.

At the moment, there was a slick layer of dried blood on its blade. It was rare that he allowed himself to take pleasure in his work. Work was work, whether a man plowed a field, roped cattle, or stocked shelves in a store. Indulging in frivolity only slowed a man down and in Pietro's line of work slowing down for even a heartbeat could get him killed.

But every now and then, when the work was done, every man deserved to stop and savor the fruits of his labors. Pietro ran his finger along the edge of the blade, touching the blood and rubbing it between his fingers.

That kill had been exceptional. Nobody had seen it

coming until it was already done. Pietro nodded in satisfaction at a job well done.

Adams had done his best to find him and failed. Another job well done.

Pietro felt a lightness in his chest.

Pride.

The smile that had barely taken root upon his scarred face was immediately straightened out and shortened into a blunt line. He took hold of the knife, nothing but a tool, and stabbed it into his leg just above the knee.

Pride was a killer of killers.

Pietro stared straight ahead until the pride was purged from his mind. The pain was there, but just barely. To make sure he accomplished what he was after, he moved the tip of the blade around a little until it scraped against the thick scars left from previous times when he'd needed to bring himself down a notch.

Removing the blade, he let out a breath and examined the tip of the knife. It had only gone in less than an inch, but that had been enough.

He would take no pleasure from his next kill.

It would be done swiftly.

It would be done right.

FORTY-ONE

Clint had been offered a seat by his host, but didn't take it. He preferred to remain on his feet, ready to move the instant it became necessary. So far, however, Mister Stone seemed content to remain calm and collected while sipping his drink.

"So," Clint said. "your killer's name is Pietro."

"It is," Stone replied. "I don't know his last name. Do you?"

Clint didn't respond with so much as a shake of his head. Inside, he sifted through memories of all the names and all the gunmen he could recall. There were a few Petes in the bunch, but no Pietros, and nobody with the cunning or skill of the man that had killed Dreskind.

"And what makes you think I'd ever know him?" Clint asked, once it became clear the conversation wouldn't move on otherwise.

Stone shrugged. "I just thought a lot of you gunfighters and killers knew each other. A sort of a brotherhood, perhaps. It doesn't matter, though. He's in the chamber and ready to be fired."

"At who?"

"That's up to you, Mister Adams. I've spoken with the parties involved and made the same offer. For those who didn't realize they were involved, I informed them and made the offer as well."

"None of this makes sense to me," Clint said. "Frankly, I don't even give a damn what you're talking about anymore. Just leave the Callums alone."

"What's your interest in them?"

"They don't deserve to be hunted by a lunatic," Clint replied.

"People die every day," Stone said simply. "It's part of life."

"I don't need lessons from a dandy in an expensive suit of clothes. Just leave the Callums alone. For that matter, if I find out you've taken part in killing anyone else, I'll have to do something about it."

"What, may I ask?"

"You're a smart man," Clint said in a low, growling voice. "I'm sure you can figure it out and I'm even more sure that when it happens, you won't like it."

There was a flicker of emotion in the corner of one of Stone's eyes. It wasn't much, but it was enough to let Clint know that he'd struck a nerve. It was gone in an instant, swept away by a man accustomed to having control over himself and everything around him.

"I bet you'd change your tune if you knew what this was about," the man said.

"I doubt it."

"What if I told you there was a lot of money involved?" Stone asked.

"There always is," Clint said.

"When you were speaking to Mister Callum or any of the others he considers to be his...so called business partners—"

"You mean the men you had killed?"

Without any emotion showing in his eyes, Stone replied, "Yes. Did any of them mention a contract?"

"They did."

Inside, Clint tensed. He knew there was something about that damn contract. Something that would come to bite a whole lot of folks in the ass.

Sometimes Clint hated it when he was right.

FORTY-TWO

lint stormed into the hotel room so quickly that he forgot to let the Callums know he was coming and almost paid the price for it.

"Good God almighty, Clint Adams!" Ed hollered as he lowered the gun he was holding. "You can't come bustin' into a room like that. I damn near blew your head off!"

Ignoring the older man and the weapon in his hand, Clint asked, "Did you read that damned contract you were passing around?"

"Huh?"

"The contract. The one that caused all this mess. Did you read it?"

Scratching his head, Edward asked, "You mean the one I had drawn up to form them investors into a group?"

"That's the one."

"Well, I'm the one that had it written up, remember?" Edward said.

"Yes," Clint said while trying to keep his patience. "I remember. Did you actually read it once it was written up, though?"

"Of course!"

"All of it?"

"Well...there was a lot of legal nonsense in there that I didn't quite understand," Edward admitted, "but it seemed to be in order."

"I just got finished talking to Stone."

Jumping to attention, Edward said, "You found him? He's here?"

"Yes. He also happened to have those papers on hand. They were more than just some agreement for your group to stay together."

"Really?"

"I told you!" Sasha said. "When you got those papers together and everyone started signing them, I told you to have a lawyer check to make certain they were in order. I told him, Clint!"

"Now's not the time for this, girl!" Ed snapped at her, annoyed.

"It wasn't the time back then, either, apparently," she bit back.

"Speaking of time," Clint said, "we don't have much of it to spare. You two need to collect your things. We're getting out of here."

"Leaving?" Ed said. "Where are we going? What's this about the contract? Tell me what the hell is going on or I'm not going anywhere!"

Clint walked up to him and said, "That contract wasn't just an agreement for partners to stick together so they could purchase those mines. It was an obligation for the lot of you to purchase those mines, splitting owner-ship among you and dividing it up in equal parts in the event that one or more of you should die."

"Wait. Die?"

"Good lord," Sasha said, exasperated. "How many times have I told you to read something all the way through before you sign it?"

"I did read it!"

"And made sure you understood it!" his daughter

demanded angrily.

To that, Edward Callum could only sputter a few indistinct noises while flapping his lips and waving at her with angry hands.

Sasha ignored her frustrated father and turned to look at Clint.

"What did the contract say?" she asked.

"Just what I told you," Clint replied. "It gives ownership of those mines to the people who signed that contract. If any of them should die, the profits are divided equally among the survivors."

"How come I didn't know about this?" Edward demanded in a whine. "I'm the one who commissioned to have the damn thing drawn up."

"Stone and his lawyers pull this sort of thing all the time with all of the folks who come to him for money," Clint explained.

"And you're probably not the first one to fall for it," Sasha grumbled.

Clint stepped in before the father and daughter could take their squabbling to new heights.

"I doubt he was the first," Clint said to Sasha, but turned to Edward and added, "but these mines have turned some incredible profits and they're slowly all headed toward Stone and nobody else."

"But—but I thought I was dealing with the Mescataine Company!" Edward complained. "It's just a small outfit looking to expand!"

"One small outfit run by a man who owns dozens of small outfits," Clint said.

"And," Sasha added, "he probably got many of those companies the same way he's trying to take everything from us—by stealin' them!"

"Probably," Clint said.

Edward looked back and forth between them, trying desperately to find a ray of hope. Snapping his fingers his face suddenly brightened as he thought he'd found something. "That contract can't be legal!"

"Why not?" Clint asked.

"Because I didn't even get everyone to sign it!" Edward said triumphantly.

"That doesn't matter."

"Yeah, but maybe this doesn't have anything at all to do with the contract," Edward said desperately. "Stone's a thieving son of a bitch. Why would you believe a damn word he says?"

"Because it makes sense," Clint told him. "It's not right but it all follows suit. Out of the men that did sign, how many of them are still alive?"

"Umm...well...just me."

"And of the men that signed who aren't alive, how many of them were killed recently?"

"Uhh..." Ed's face paled and he staggered back a few steps until he could sit down on his cot. "Jesus. It's true. This is all my fault."

"No," Clint was quick to say. "You made a mistake, but this isn't your fault. Men like Stone get rich by threatening and cheating good folks like you."

"But," Sasha said, "if he hadn't bothered with some stupid piece of paper..."

Stopping her, Clint said, "It was a mistake. Plain and simple, and it's too late to do anything about it now other than what we're doing."

"I'm the last one," Ed said as if he was the only one in the room. "I'm a dead man. Those mines are worth a fortune. Stone wants them. He'll kill me for 'em. Unless...wait! That's it! I'll just sign off my share. I'll sign whatever I need to in order to get out of the deal. He can have the mines and all that money."

Clint faced him and said fiercely, "No!"

"Why? No amount of money is worth putting my little girl in danger!"

"Because it's too late to pay Stone off. He's in too deep to let one man on that contract live and even if he wasn't, he shouldn't get away with murder."

"I agree, but what else can we do?"

Clint went to the door of the room and opened it just enough to get a look out. He could see light coming in through the open front door on the first floor and a young man hurry inside.

After closing the door, he said, "What we do is finish this right here and now." With that, he went to the window on the other side of the room, opened it, and leapt over the sill.

FORTY-THREE

This killer, the man Stone called Pietro, wasn't after glory or another man's reputation. He was a lurker and had proven as much several times over already. He found a spot where he couldn't be seen, waited for orders, and struck when he was least expected. And so, instead of trying to see him or guess where the next blow would be delivered, Clint was there when the orders were given. Or, by presenting himself as a target to Stone during their little conversation, caused the order to be given soon after he left.

He figured Pietro was nearby, but couldn't just storm around looking for him. Even a quiet search would most likely be spotted and Pietro would slither away to a darker corner. Clint guessed the killer was holed up in one of the neighboring tents or possibly in one of the other rooms of his hotel. There were only two rooms on the second floor and Clint knew who was in them. There were two rooms on the first floor, one of which didn't have a window, making coming or going quietly that much more difficult. Therefore, if Pietro was in the hotel, he would be in the room on the left and directly beneath Edward and Sasha's.

Stone was absolutely right when he said the only reason things hadn't been a lot bloodier for Clint was because Pietro hadn't been ordered to kill him. Clint changed that by threatening Stone and his operation, presenting himself as the next target. After that, he just needed to wait for someone to pass the order on to Pietro. Clint recognized the young man who'd hurried into the hotel through the front door as one of the men near the Mescataine offices. If that man was here, it most likely meant he had to deliver a message.

It was something of a gamble when Clint jumped from the second floor window to land in front of the window on the first floor. Still, there was only so much groundwork to be set before he was buried in it. Instincts should be trusted. Risks needed to be taken. A venomous snake like Pietro had to be taken by surprise.

Judging by the look on the killer's face when he spun around to get a look out his window, Clint accomplished his goal.

Not wanting to waste a fraction of the moment he'd bought himself, Clint drew his Colt and used it to smash the window in front of him.

"Thought I'd save you the trouble of coming up all those stairs," he said.

No man deserved to be gunned down without a chance to defend himself. Not even a slimy reptile like Pietro. That, after all, was what separated men from assassins.

Pietro snapped one arm out to slap a hand against the chest of the young man who'd been sent by Stone. Pushing the younger man back, Pietro had a clear range of sight and motion as he used his other hand to send a skinny blade through the air. The knife sliced through the short distance between Pietro and Clint, shaving a sliver of meat from Clint's shoulder as it passed. If Clint hadn't been quick enough to turn sideways, away from the deadly knife, it would have been lodged deep in his chest.

Squeezing his trigger, Clint fired into the hotel room. A spray of blood hit the wall behind Pietro, but the killer didn't give any indication that he was hit. Instead, he reached for the door behind him and took a step toward the hall.

The instant Clint vaulted over the sill and through the window, he knew that Pietro's backward step had been a ruse. Like a boxer feinting with a left jab, Pietro meant to follow up with another punch coming in the opposite direction. Despite being shot, Pietro moved quickly enough to launch himself at Clint before Clint was all the way inside the room. In his hand, Pietro held a small .32 which had been hidden somewhere on his person.

Two shots blasted through the room.

The first came from Pietro and had been fired in a rush.

The second came from Clint, who'd squeezed his trigger in mid-jump.

When Clint's boots touched down upon the floor inside Pietro's room, the fight was over. Pietro's momentum still carried him to Clint but the killer's eyes were glazing over. Clint grabbed the front of Pietro's shirt to keep him from dropping.

"Should have stuck to running away from me," Clint said to the assassin. "Suited you a whole lot more."

He then released his grip and allowed Pietro to fall. Even the killer's final breath was silent.

Clint looked up from the body at his feet while bringing the Colt up as well. Standing in front of him was the young man who'd been outside the Mescataine tent when he'd left after his conversation with Stone. It was such a quick meeting that Clint didn't know if the guy was another partner or just someone who brought Stone his coffee.

"I—I'm just a messenger," the young man sputtered.

"That's perfect," Clint said, while stepping forward to shove him out of the room. "Then let's go and deliver a message."

FORTY-FOUR

The first person to step into the tent used by the Mesca-taine Company was the younger fellow who'd been sent to Pietro's room. When he saw him arrive, Stone was standing over the table in the middle of the enclosed space with Hobart and Jeremy directly across from him.

"Ah," Stone said pleasantly. "I take it our bit of business is concluded?"

"Yes," Clint said as he stepped in behind the younger man. "It is. Your assassin is dead and the Callums are hereby released from that contract."

Unaffected by the news of Pietro's death, Stone replied, "You can take their place. Get rid of Edward Callum, do what you want with the daughter and you can share in the profits of those mines."

"I'll tell you what I told you the last time you made that offer," Clint said. "No."

"Fine," Stone said as he turned his back to Clint and snapped his fingers at the two men closest to him. "Kill both of these men."

"What?" the younger messenger cried while holding his hands in front of him as if to deflect any incoming gunfire.

Hobart was the first to draw and Jeremy wasn't far behind. They squared their shoulders to the front door and raised their pistols. Before either man's gun was lifted more than an inch above their holsters, Clint burned them down with three quick shots fired from the hip. Two drilled through Hobart's chest and the third punched a third eye in Jeremy's forehead.

Pointing the smoking Colt at Stone, Clint said, "You can put an end to this business one of two ways. The first is you signing over all of those mines to everyone else on that contract. The dead men's families get their share while the living have theirs."

Scowling as if the prospect of losing profit was the most distasteful thing to have happened over the last several days, Stone bent down to snatch the pistol from Jeremy's dead hand. Clint waited for him to stand up again. He even gave Stone a chance to change his mind before taking his shot. When Stone lifted the pistol and took aim, Clint dropped the businessman with a single bullet through the heart.

"And that," Clint said while turning to face the last surviving member of the Mescataine Company, "is the second way to conclude this business. What about you, friend?" he said to the messenger. "Care to start any business of your own?"

The young man raised his hands, shook his head, and bolted from the tent.

Clint smirked and holstered his Colt. "That's the smartest move anyone's made in this whole damn deal."

*****

"Do you have to leave?" Sasha asked.

They were standing outside of Callum Parts & Supply. He'd already said goodbye to her father inside.

"Yep," he said, "it's time for me to be moving on."

"Is that what you always do?" she asked. "Move on?"

He stroked the Darley Arabian's neck and said to her, "Eclipse and I don't usually stay in one place for very long."

She folded her arms and shrugged.

"I guess I'm stuck here," she said. "With Dad."

"Get him to leave."

"Are you kidding?" she asked. "As long as he thinks there's gold..."

"Then you leave," he said.

"And go where?"

It was his turn to shrug.

"Anywhere else, Sasha," he said. "Or, at least, some place cleaner than this."

"That's probably not a bad idea," she said, "sometime in the future."

"Well then," he said, "goodbye."

She pecked him on the cheek and watched with her arms folded as he mounted up and rode away.

ABOUT THE AUTHOR

As "J.R. Roberts" Bob Randisi is the creator and author of the long running western series, *The Gunsmith*. Under various other pseudonyms he has created and written the "Tracker," "Mountain Jack Pike," "Angel Eyes," "Ryder," "Talbot Roper," "The Son of Daniel Shaye," and "the Gamblers" Western series. His western short story collection, *The Cast-Iron Star and Other Western Stories*, is now available in print and as an ebook from Western Fictioneers Books.

In the mystery genre he is the author of the *Miles Jacoby, Nick Delvecchio, Gil & Claire Hunt, Dennis McQueen, Joe Keough*, and *The Rat Pack*, series. He has written more than 500 western novels and has worked in the Western, Mystery, Sci-Fi, Horror and Spy genres. He is the editor of over 30 anthologies. All told he is the author of over 650 novels. His arms are very, very tired.

He is the founder of the Private Eye Writers of America, the creator of the Shamus Award, the co-founder of Mystery Scene Magazine, the American Crime Writers League, Western Fictioneers and their Peacemaker Award.

In 2009 the Private Eye Writers of America awarded him the Life Achievement Award, and in 2013 the Readwest Foundation presented him with their President's Award for Life Achievement.

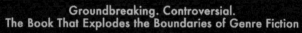